ALSO BY JOSEPH McELROY

Women and Men

Plus

Lookout Cartridge

Ancient History: A Paraphase

Hind's Kidnap: A Pastoral on Familiar Airs

A Smuggler's Bible

The Letter Left to Me

The Letter Left to Me

A NOVEL BY

JOSEPH McELROY

Alfred A. Knopf   New York   1988

THIS IS A BORZOI BOOK
PUBLISHED BY ALFRED A. KNOPF, INC.

Copyright © 1988 by Joseph McElroy
All rights reserved under International and Pan-American Copyright Conventions.
Published in the United States by Alfred A. Knopf, Inc., New York,
and simultaneously in Canada by Random House of Canada Limited, Toronto.
Distributed by Random House, Inc., New York.

A portion of this book first appeared in *Conjunctions*.

Library of Congress Cataloging-in-Publication Data
McElroy, Joseph.
The letter left to me.
I. Title.
PS3563.A293L4   1988   813'.54   88–45222
ISBN 0–394–57196–7

Manufactured in the United States of America
First Edition

The Letter Left to Me

i

The woman holding, then handing over the letter to this poised, dumbfounded fifteen-year-old: is the letter also *hers*? She's been busy, her hands are anything but idle here in a room of a city apartment, but today what belongs to her hands? The words are echoey-bare—a room, a city apartment—they sound rugless, not yet moved-*in,* don't they?—which is not this place at all.

My father has written a letter to me, a letter *for* me. He isn't here—which is the way with letters, I think (like an alarm signaling my distraction from whatever I ought to be thinking about). But this letter *has* been here. How long? (I'm building backwards naturally.) Was it waiting for him to be not here? It's been in a drawer of the desk right here in the living room, that open lower drawer there.

A drop-leaf desk made by an early-nineteenth-century cousin of my mother's. I would sit and lean my elbow on it—write a letter, say, that I'd been reminded of more than once—though I don't forget things—a thank-you note—which could have been why I wrote it at my parents' desk, on the spur maybe of being asked again. This desk reacted to me with an experienced give but a subtle solidity in its joints and grooves and finished sockets, its dark-glossed grains. To close it up, with its pigeonholes and miniature drawers, you raise the drop leaf. So its underside, with a tiny brass lock that shines like gold, becomes the front panel banked into a groove along the edge of the mantel-like top. A china vase—orange, with two or three flowers in it, and nearly taken for granted by me—stands on that top surface, which, I see, roofs the pigeonholes below whether the desk is open *or* closed.

But when was it not open? I would put my hand under the drop leaf and find the dingy key where it hung half-turned in the lock and I would lift the drop leaf and close the desk and slide the two narrow boards that had been supporting the drop leaf in out of sight except for their brass knobs, and I would work the lock. The desk was not kept locked. The lower drawers had locks, too, but this same key.

Did my mother know of my father's letter?

She didn't need to say a thing getting up from the desk lightly and alone and turning to me in the same just and dis-covering motion. (*I* knew what must be in the envelope.) When she wouldn't normally have *gotten* up. Though might turn half-way toward me in her *chair* as if a part of *her,* natural and questioning, had come into the room.

She didn't need to say a thing. And it's as *if* she didn't. The January winds off the harbor ripple certain windowpanes, the living room paled around us half-wittingly. My impatience I keep hidden, it is mean and my own. This open lower drawer of the desk tilts downward full of folders. Jammed-looking is what it is—inner monument to record keeping, this weighty, rather beloved (at the moment) drawer, stricken, threatening because of being temporarily just left pulled out. She's terribly energetically systematic, she is managing, but so finely that it is like silence or an absence similar to that. Who was it called me "poised"? Someone—a woman who didn't know my father and came to the funeral because of my mother.

My mother hands over the envelope and I feel her. What happens now? Is it already in our living with each other? Nothing's up to me unless I think I can now have anything I want. I am standing *with* her; this is about all I am doing. I'm sure it's some deal between us, she'll do her part. I could be on stilts assimilating into this living room where she is; but I'm the one this envelope is meant for. Am I to make something of my "envelope" now?

She sees that I get my envelope. We live here; but this is an appointment, her voice out here in the living room a minute ago called my name, it had me in mind in part: I thought of whole intentions outside me, of penalty, the floor plan, her voice when she sings.

But that summoning sound of activity elsewhere turns out to be honor, not fresh danger days and hours after my father's amazing death. For when I call, "Yes?" and locomote briskly from my room into the living room, I get this envelope.

Is it some paper of release, Graduation a year and a half ahead of time? (But my diploma when the time comes will be like everybody else's, and this isn't the headmaster, grizzled, pink-cheeked, a "Doctor.") This dear woman and I are unbalanced equals; I might spell it out. My living, wildly valued mother. As I take the envelope, my thumb below my name, I just pick up elsewhere on the envelope her hand, her fingers leaving it.

Fingers of someone else. And her *husband* has just about vanished. He is "no more no more." He is gone. A goner! What about it? I have the words, some; and I can say I loved and admired my father. (I "wished him well," if I am to be listened to.)

In the living room, the first day of the letter, I don't want to be *in* this silence of his. But then I do—I know it, I know that much. It's closer than my mother's waiting scent, his absence, the dumb plummet of his absence. Closer upon me than my clothes—this brown corduroy shirt I got for Christmas that I like so much I can practically settle for it. The room lives with her own near scent, clean, speaks it, or holds it, it is *about* her, I wouldn't know what it is, it isn't just "scent" or soap, I might name it like an olfactory microscoper. I know *his* smells, I kiss his cheek. But what *is* his smell? Now lost to this room, these cold windows, he who liked "the way" my mother "lived."

Words better than mine into the phone to a woman friend of my mother's calling to see "how he's doing"—three, four days ago (what's fast and what slow here?). And I said, "My father passed away last night." *I* who of all people know enough to say "died": yet said "passed away." I'm on the phone, I feel that person's good surprise, the push of her spirit at *my* end of the line—welcome her wide, generous mouth!—a musician calling from "out of town," her eyes easy, strong (lazy? happily remembering sleep?), her heavy gray hair created with big veins of black color, which are hair too. Curly bangs, bang curls upon her forehead; last summer's coarse, tanned throat and blue work shirt, too: a *musician* (the skill and beauty in that do take your mind); a confident, pointed force of a person but less quick on the phone the other night; a *blunt* "nice person"—"hard," it comes to me—who gave me a message for my mother, said things to *me*, says my mother's first name to me, *and* doesn't ask to *speak* to my mother. This fleshly woman-voice, her husband was my mother's mentor once upon a time, bushy-haired conducting in a summer barn in Massachusetts and crazy in a way about tuning up and "making music" and telling others what to do.

I've come through those quite powerful words I had with his wife, phone call's over and done with, one of many, a sort of business; so now three days or so after I broke the news to the friend of my mother's powerfully, I finger the long-size business envelope, it has my father's voice in it, I fear. Never mind *passed away* (my mother wouldn't say that either—but my father's family *would*, I see, as if those ready words, loathed and officious as I spoke them, *relieved* us of words). Yet words *in* me: "passed away": maybe he hasn't "died." I'll bet he has.

My father is not so much dead as not living. Or not here. This sizable room was sometimes his—reading, reading so well, so sweepingly, books, flipping pages; aiming his frown, commanding himself, one trousered leg crossed over the other, his black shoe stirring from something going on in him, like a smile: for he, and not only he, can smile as he *frowns*. When it is the newspaper he's reading, his head moves defendingly, welcomingly, strategically at large in the scope of the shoulder-wide page and its columns: I can tell he's looking at a picture, I come behind the couch, it's a photo of a Jap atrocity, I put my hands on him, the molded shoulder padding, he's home from work, bending over him I smell his sweet daylong scalp.

I've seen lunatics stand in this room. Beside furniture somehow. A wing chair to the elbow, lampshade to the tits, coffee table to the shin, drop leaf to the fly. I'm measuring the room as ours, my mother's and mine. Standing is one thing people do in the living room. Its size has a spirit, too, a room with openings into other rooms.

I am inside and at least get the idea that I could be standing outside. If she gave it to me, the envelope is mine. Mine to open anyway.

We're polite. But every few hours she's different, too, amid my father's death, which schedules everything to perfection and puts yesterday on top of tomorrow if I try to think when things happened, though I don't at all think her different when all has stopped or has left us as if she would now be just her.

Yesterday cooks a moistly good-to-look-at meal "with her left hand" practically, as *he* noted her airy motions at dinnertime: food heals the insides where my *father* is, actually—oh, "helpings" we say are "generous." She gets it onto the dining-room table with my help; doesn't tell me to sit up straight, I'm hungry politely in my *father's* place; and I speak, and she nods with a blind courtesy, or such learning nearness—and I'm at a loss facing her reserved grief, scared, tempted by it; talks with me, we can't believe the "behavior" of an elderly battle-axe by marriage who showed up late to drive with us to my father's church for the funeral, griped about my mother's directions, condemned the trip over here from Manhattan, the subway ride that had been full of doubt (who was twenty-three years in China, her late husband my mother's cousin with Standard Oil, and now doesn't have a husband to have a funeral *for* or children to bury her—quite separate from all others, it came to me yesterday at the table as our interesting meal went on and it came to me that we had eaten alone together often). My mother will talk on the phone out in the hall and I can hear her not exclude me, she says "we"; she's been writing at the desk, I'm afraid to see her cry as if she has no right to, and I have not seen her cry.

What will we do now standing in the living room? We would take a trip, my mother said at the hospital, a cruise, when "this" was "over": he had "improved"; it was two days before he died.

But what will we do *now*, standing in the living room? I know, apparently—for I don't *feel* I *don't* know. I'm half *free*. You have time to spend with this. I am hearing a lot about what you do at a time like this. You live through it. You go on. You do things. I give some of it back, saying things and *hearing* things as if I've known them before. Yet am a distinguished personage right now and don't care. I am "doing my part." She lets me know this in looks more unspeakable and businesslike than sentimentally approving—yet presently recalled as unyieldingly tender, dryly like the faintest down upon her cheekbones.

I'm building, but backwards naturally. As if this envelope upon being passed to the dumbfounded, poised fifteen-year-old is passed right back, because anything can happen if you don't know what it means. Shouldn't my mother and I open it together?

Or, standing here in the living room with an envelope in my hand, I'm free in one breath like I've achieved an unquestionable thing so beyond my *known* gifts that people in my vicinity go along with their awe in the event. Yet it's no more than entering a room to join some friends of my parents having drinks after church, and a man with a silly thought smiling on his face tells me out of the blue, "You should go to law school." Why was my father not there? He came late, from services at *his* church in another part of Brooklyn. She is a beautiful—my father said she was "a beautiful woman" and he was right—beautiful legs, "slim" (slim-*boned,* I would think for myself perhaps while he was actually talking), "tall" (which means "tall for a woman"), very dark-haired but not dark, sometimes a reserved person (come to think of it), my mother, very often so charmingly welcoming she's not generous at *all* but maybe just enjoys it. A kind person ("soul") like my father. What she did for "others." He was also stern (in his quickness) with a gentleness unwavering that could have scared me I almost grasp with the envelope and its contents in my hand held not low at thigh level or high near my face like something to talk with but at belt level: wasn't *she* some of these things? but no punster or connoisseur of slips of the tongue like him, or light quoter of things that stayed with me or I let them. "A daydreamer," he called me, speaking to another man in this living room, with me here, so I knew he had thought it before. I *saw* he had.

Maybe now she is different. (But this can't occur to me slowly and sort of fully even now when she's what she is just to me without my father to see her.) With people she's *not* reserved sometimes. Yet I don't especially know this—don't much bring it to mind standing beside her in the living room with the unchanged but comfortably empty furniture: equals, equals through being of different *bodies,* I think this is what my fingers dream moist and casual on the envelope—client/lawyer, *that* was it, but *she's* the one that needs the lawyer—and *has two*!

There's going to be more breathing room in the apartment before long but there's less now, the thought's already gone from me, for *I* go on. The light from the view is very smart light, too smart for me, her hands don't touch me, I have this envelope from my *father.* I don't know it's from my father. My mother has said, I think this was from your father. A trace of novelty outlines my skin or heart. A shiver of wit, once my father's, offers to cloak me. "Less noise from the cheap seats," it means not noise primarily, it means you don't have as much right to speak, you're young ("to say the least"). The two of *them* could be loud. Or "silly" *they* called it. A reaching, breaking laughter I happily received from my room, shouted all together at a dinner party by them and their friends and then names nearly shouted, as if for minutes on end the words I couldn't really hear in between these bursts equaled a grownup surprise-party game of silence until it couldn't be contained.

But the two of *them* weren't *wild*-loud, or loud-awful, and were admirably silly, I grasped. They "get me up" to listen to the Joe Louis fight: as if I am going in at ten o'clock to see it, a two-man (two-name) fate glittering with night, the sheerly bright living room like new weight, and the distance of a radio voice's closeness, all reported bit by bit to us who were not there with an unfolding and building and completeness of waking life, which, coming to it from bed away from this group of relaxed grownups, smelling of comfortably spicy stinky sweet drinks and smoke, I felt to be reliably thrilling, "explosive" but bleeding, or bruised, but not cruel.

Joe Louis runs his words together as if he's talking fast in the interview after the fight. He says hello to his ma, she wasn't there, she was far away listening to the radio, the grownups laughed in a friendly way, they said, *H'lo, Ma.*

The fight was an execution in its high preparation and late-night time, in my garishly awake state an entertaining side of tomorrow which I had gone some distance toward already in sleep: still, a right given me by my parents jointly, in return for Sleep First, and I never could sleep (I thought) from seven-thirty until ten, but more or less did, and woke up fast, *part* of me, as if nothing held me back for a time—I wanted my father to be happy, I always knew—and an hour later went back to bed and to sleep readily, the champion visible and quiet, hardly out of breath, amid the announcer's voice, voices near the announcer, things I could see from listening to him, not from my father and the guests commenting knowingly. The Brown Bomber looked less big in newspaper pictures, it was his smooth-shaped proportions.

It was a relief that Louis had won again. It was excellent. I went back to my room myself and slept. My mother let them talk, I felt, she's smiling, and smiling so sociably, lovably, entertainingly, or bringing in someone's glass. He liked the way she *lived. She* told me once that was what he had said. All the rooms are hers. Also hers and mine.

What do my mother and I do *different* today, this envelope in my hand? It's back to regular life, is it? But today it's a cold late-January morning, and my mother didn't have to say it—but then I figure she did—that it's from my father.

The envelope isn't birthday money from an uncle; or to be greeted like Christmas. It isn't my birthday. It is January. ("Your *envelope*"—"your Christmas envelope"—"I have your Christmas envelope upstairs," she said to the doorman Christmas Eve afternoon because he would be going off duty. He has grayish silver stripes, two, just above the cuffs of his grayish-green uniform jacket sleeves. It might be just an envelope, "*your* envelope"! My father was upstairs reading in his slippers and his bathrobe and regular clothes, alive.) Christmas was with my *father*; so it seems cheatingly months ago; but no it doesn't, it's recent, his voice is around somewhere, like Christmas: wrapping paper, slashing, ripping (yet care, polite love in the glad suspicion of "I *won*der what *this* is") to the scent of pine branches, the aroma of sausages, coffee (which only my mother drinks), her unusually crisp buckwheat cakes that don't get soggy in syrup (How do you make them like this? my father said with his mouth full. Oh, with my left hand, my mother says)—and the two-second gasp of silence as the "loot" is exposed. (It's *just* what I *wan*ted!, or she, You shouldn't have—it's beautiful.)

I'm electrified—he's in it.

Rip it open, find out what he wrote, what he said—what am I waiting for? It may be for all of us. It has my name on the envelope. I have to open it. Names aren't changing. He wrote a letter to me—*for* me—to be left for me. He left a letter. The letter is given to me three or four days after he died. She has done the job of getting it to me and I should open it here. She handed it to me. *You shouldn't have,* I think.

I have it; so my father left this for me. (I know what it is.) I'm *called* by my name on the envelope: my two initials and "last" name, and the "Jr."

This letter was typed. I *see* him typing but then I don't. I don't think he *ever* typed. I typed from the time I was seven. I should know if he did. He worked in an office high up in Wall Street, wrote figures and words in pencil on lined pads. "Tablets" the stationery store sometimes calls them. They got to be like books. He doesn't tear the sheets off them, or *I* never saw him; and they thickened with his writing. Did someone else type "up" this letter? I can't think so. What's the right thing to do? Time is fidgeting, according to my father.

Did my mother know of my father's letter? Maybe I will ask her. When was it written? I will never place anything on top of it. It was never mailed. There's no postmark, no stamp. The sender is not far away.

Together we think he was a good man and I am lucky.

What is outside the room comes back and was always there. I believe that's true—thinking that way—but not coming out with it is a little like not thinking it, but it can't be.

The solid paper of the envelope on my fingers, from where we stand for a moment or two my mother and I have the embracing distances of the inner harbor, sights belonging to us if we wanted them. Right out the front windows. The Battery at the lower end (this end, where you can tell Manhattan's an island) right in front of us across the East River—large-scale, not-to-be-*trusted* nearness. "Battery" as in "stored electrical energy" (I decided). The ferry terminals low-scaled on their piers point outward—they *are* their piers. We have piers on this side, freighters loading, loading what?—for South America. I'm supposed to do something with the letter. *Have* it, maybe. Across the river, edifices of the Wall Street financial enclave gather tally, where my father went to work. Noble and subtle or thin and to be taken for granted, and unlike landscape not graspably all there, those buildings are not "fine" as *people* were said to be "fine." As my *father,* who's now become the writer of this letter, was called "nicest man," and "fine," and ("to say the least") "*gentle*man" (a man in good clothes, black Chesterfield, velvet collar—lifting his hat—a derby, black and velvety hard—stiff-brimmed—on the street).

The *colors* here become ours, they're like *her,* like my mother: calm upholstery pine-green; the soft dull reds (found also among the chalks I draw with in my room somewhat messily but draw less and less); lemony greens of morning—and of *choice,* it comes to me somewhat foolishly; and pink that's really not pink because it's darkened by dusty light inside the cloth; and *dark* green that sends my eyes, my hands, to dark wood carved and used as if mined richly; and patterns in strong silk. The room is hers, she did this. My father didn't make this living room at all. But my mother made this living room for not just my father and her; yet anyway did it alone, I now see. She will "entertain" in it.

The room holds the size it had but not the paint smell when it was being "decorated" a year and more ago before my mother and father moved in.

The view swung past the Statue clear to The Narrows, where the outer harbor waited. "The Narrows" is what my father calls it. Then looking around to the right with ease, we love pointlessly the Brooklyn Bridge. Though we looked beyond it.

Bounded by this grandeur, my mother's the *silent* arguer, stubborn, and delicately so, more something than I know. Others' words she might want to share—the poetry, the words, she is a poet, or poetic, *I* know, but would not come out much with old story-memories. She would seem to warmly bear the enthusiasm of others, nod with pursed-lip jollity and actual warmth at what came out of their mouths at the sights from our living-room windows, the vision of Wall Street right over there, choppy waters, the Statue at night, the Bridge. She will warm to *jokes,* I will tell her a couple when I get home from school, and she secretly with a potential unpleasantness insisted on humor. I don't know if I should read her the letter here and now.

Whatever *I* decide. She didn't get one.

She did not wear a veil at his funeral. She is a "widow." That's not young enough to suit her. I think of saying with the letter in my hand, Well, let's see what he's been doing—maybe he's got some news! "Woman" sounds in this slowness of the pause of my father's death, not "gal," which the women of her acquaintance will say with a casual vim comradely not so much with one another as with their whole set.

I don't know how to put it, how to get from here to my room with my letter. Time isn't short at all, but I'm stupid, I'm a dead duck: I think of him coming back, not *right* back, but it's how I happen to feel. We're looking at the letter, the thing in my hand, not each other.

My thumbnail below my name, I turned the envelope over

and ran my thumb up under the flap, and I slit the envelope raggedly, methodically open with my finger. I opened the two sheets of paper and they are typed, and there's my name.

The contents were in his mind, his eyes in *front* of his mind. I feel his handwriting, his "hand." In mine.

I speak. And in my armpits to a heart on each side close to these touchy ribs comes a thought from my mother, not in words—only its twoness comes in that minute of attachment; it was maybe that love was "only" this or that—which I so can't imagine her voicing, that I *believe* it as a dangerously clear act *un*said, some sentimental vying.

The letter is dated February 22—why, it's Washington's Birthday! The letter's been in the house for months, well hasn't it? Months of his *life*. But three years ago almost! Here all the time. He had it, he might have gone and looked at it, recalled it, opened it, he's taking action but taking his time: what was *I* doing? it was still his, his fingers took it out, unfolded it, stretched it taut, he did not scrunch it and lob it into the waste-basket that's covered in red leather embossed in gold like my bookends.

A line waits, two lines, they terribly ask something of me, or nothing, for he won't speak out loud again, I saw them, I might know them at a glance. I am afraid. That after all he *is* dead. To this my mother who does love me would say in gentle embarrassment, No—the way *her* mother used to say, Pshaw. *And* I could take it or leave it; or think I am not about to read it standing here or read it aloud. And they are *not* "lines."

I take in a *few* lines. My father's been dead three days or so, I don't for a moment know how many days. I think "*been* dead." I don't sit down, I don't read it. My mother's twin thoughts do exist, and somewhere in me they are to do with the letter being in my hand.

Now, on the day my mother has given me the envelope, I see that Gertie comes Thursdays: because my mother said, Are you going back to school tomorrow? Gertie's coming. The letter might as well hold the answer to her question—but why *ask* me? Gertie comes every week, our not really Negro cleaning lady, small, busy, softly quick-talking, with glasses, part Shinnecock Indian. I once called her "ma'am," trying it out wrongly. I am never here at the moment her key in the lock softly cracks the silence of the faraway front door. Come to clean "the house," run the wash through the machines and the wringers in the basement, and at the end of the day iron swiftly under the ceiling light in the kitchen; before she changes her "costume" (it occurs to me), puts on her overcoat while my mother, so much taller, pours two somewhat statuesque slender cut-glass glasses of sherry from the dining-room decanter and they have a chat. My mother puts *her* glass on the enamel top of the stove, doing things. Just two *women* I fleetingly interest myself "thinking," the tall one standing, the small one seated. Family tribulations Gertie summarizes not in stories, the organ they've collected money to buy for her minister may not materialize, he may devote the money to some other purpose. Gertie ties her kerchief; it enshrines her cheeks. She is respectfully affectionate, is loyal, unquestioningly loyal is what I see I face.

But my mother has asked if I'm going back to school tomorrow, and Of *course* I am is the answer, and the letter has nothing to do with it. This is a woman who's handed me the letter. O.K., let's find out what he's been doing—find out his news! (But since when?)

But I took it away to my room, it and its envelope, he kept his torn-open envelopes with the letters in them.

I tried to read the letter slowly and it meant *too* much. I might be building something that's built, and wouldn't *that* be stupid. My forearms on my thighs, somewhat powerfully alone sitting on the edge of the bed—like sitting on the john—I'm reading with not much language of my own loose and sounding in my head—with a dramatic horror at this potential Victrola

record, and with relief in the action, with fearless trivial hope—
yet what can I do? I learned, I taught myself, to read, to read
this page in two hands, the suspense wasn't killing me, I got up
and went and closed the door.

My eyeballs became sore and hot. My face retched. It retched
across its bones and life, eye sockets, pointless and hopeless. My
face closed and opened with grateful helplessness. Sitting on the
bed in the same position, I wept over that letter. I was in my
room. I dripped on the paper. I held it in front of me. I had
his voice and *had* had it. "In retrospect I am appalled by my
neglect of the vistas which life has opened to me." My thoughts
caroused. He would not knock. And I became *interested*. If my
father had gone back to take another look, he'd have had to slit
open the envelope and then use a new one. But he didn't need
to lick the envelope to begin with. Did he show it to *her*? I
believe he didn't.

She will still read to me. But will read letters or amusing
newspaper items, a birth at the zoo, or a rave review of a play
that may make her voice quaver with sentiment—will read to
me in the kitchen or in the living room. To my father she will
read in the living room and the bedroom. He'll say, "Let's have
a little light on the subject." There's more going on in his mind.

I had plenty of time, unless there was a thing I must do at
once. I'm sitting, he's gone. I know that I don't know what's
quite happened to me. Which meant it had to be more than
my father dying; because I did know that that had happened.
Others act like they know what's going on. I accepted what had
happened like a dope. ("You dope," he said out on the street,
when I had left something home, a jabbing humor as if we were
a larger family.) The violinist on the phone the night after my
father died gave me a message for my mother, that she's thinking
of her, she "loved" my father—when we come to Connecticut
they have a dog now, a "too large bear-sized mutt" they found
sleeping on a mountain. Did this woman on the *phone* know

what had happened therefore?—when *I* was only *acting* as if I knew? I swear I felt no one else knew either. But not as some failure in them. I "knew" all this with a decided clearness of ignorance accepted by me. It was a little thrill to weep. Cry, weep—it was spasms or really gluts lifting from my stomach region down to my wretchedly ready legs. My door would never be knocked on and still I was alert to it and to the hall outside because it might be my father coming to knock and to say my name. But not while I'm reading his letter.

It said my name. It expressed the hope that I would make the most of my abilities as he said he had failed to do. It identified the two things he could leave me. A healthy constitution was one; a good education was the other. From the very first dreadful, instinctive, true time through, I could tell he was asking of me something in his *absence*. Do I mean "hard work"? The weight of this letter's gift is its giver's real absence. I will tell my mother when I come out of my room that it is a fine letter. Then I will give it to her. Or I'll say nothing and look into her eyes like a hug.

My father cited Abraham Lincoln. Lincoln made me sad here. He was himself. My father included among Lincoln's achievements "in the face of adversity" having succeeded despite being married to "an impossible woman."

I had read about Mary Todd Lincoln, I'm sure, and heard about her; I had seen her in a movie, her eyes oval, awfully dark, a small, intent person—best movie I'd ever seen, with "a story to tell," as my father once said of a musical he and my mother went to.

My parents and I went to Washington. The Supreme Court opened inward like a church, glitteringly bespectacled justices far away but right there exhibited for the few minutes we stood just looking. My father said I'm to keep a notebook, the cherry blossoms will be out, I imagine them red, we'll be away four days beyond the week of my vacation. Neat-domed, the Jefferson

Memorial was new. I didn't actually write down how the seated Lincoln's knees were like cliffs but real knees with bones.

At Gettysburg it got cold. George Pickett's Virginian division lost three-quarters of its men—the skinny guide didn't stop talking to take a breath—until my father couldn't wait any longer and asked where the corrals for the battery horses had been, but it was a question the guide didn't really know the answer to. Getting into the car, my father called him an "old geezer," and my mother gave a delayed, low-pitched laugh starting the car and looking to see if there was anything behind us so I thought, What was she thinking the moment before she laughed?, I thought it was a mysterious liking for my father. In my desk drawer is a cardboard box of paper clips and an eraser in the shape of a parallelogram; and in the same drawer a dented, powder-seared shell from Pickett's Charge nailed to a little block of grimy pine. I am only remembering him.

He must have thought about his death. He said in his will that he might die before I reached "maturity." My mother showed me the will one day, *gave* it, it seemed, to me—to read, to take *away* and read. How personal his prediction seemed, or how reliable. A will wasn't like a talk. My father's great vim (which could flag abruptly, calmly) was the vim of a *reliable* man.

My letter *had* been in the safe-deposit box, I learned from my mother; but it had been "found" by her in the living-room desk. She knew the envelope.

It was him; I felt his voice.

I was overmatched, yet with an answering privilege that I picked up just holding the letter, sitting privately on my bed with my feet on the rug. When do I *do* something with this? My face feels this crying with a relief of crying itself more than interest. It's my gift, I don't try to remember it. It is a story told. Or is it hard to remember? I've read it again and again. I love it. It ends like a story.

... try to remember that, however keen the disappointments of youth may seem, there is nothing as bitter as
a middle-aged man's realization that—

I could hardly get through the next words, I feel I have been
told a whole life, and I do not want the letter to end. So much
talk goes on, and this ends—this always ends. In grief, maybe
I know grief is "about" remembering a middle-aged man's realization. But how am I going to do *that*? I want him here.
What have I without him here? I felt for myself that he was
more light *and* I mean more swiftly smart than other grownup
men, and never-turning-away friendly. Coming home along the
street in early evening and greeting me across the street where
I'm playing, alive to me but not taking me away from my friends.
I happened to see him race a man along a bathhouse boardwalk
once, I was still in my bathing suit, splintery thin boards under
my feet and grains of sand. But he is dressed, his dark blue
trunks just visible rolled in his towel, and without warning, his
body dropped lower, or his hips and haunches; it was not a
straining sprint like mine, it covered the ground in one rush
and he was dangerously laughing on the spur of the moment
like loud breaths of power; and happening to come barefoot
round a corner, I saw him with these others.

He was capable of being nervous, but was not jumpy, as *I*
see him. His aliveness came my way in near-complete attention
moderated by its everlasting thought but by patented seriousness
going on here *and* elsewhere.

He plays lacrosse at college and afterward on a nationally
important team in Brooklyn; I easily see him, I probably waste
time seeing him, running like blazes down the sideline all by
himself, like a joke, absorbed, but he is not alone, he knows
where everybody is, and then down there he reaches up his stick,
snaring out of a higher layer of air a long pass into the corner,
twisting his stick to hold the ball and centering it all in one

catapulting hammer-motion so the ball bends back across toward the goal and my father's teammate and the goalie who has come out too far hit in midair and the ball is somewhere else, loose, taken by someone else, who is sometimes on one team, sometimes on the other.

He had rheumatic fever as a child (a boy)—was there reliability in *that*? It left him with slight (I am always told) heart trouble and there was a "slight" defect in his heart that was referred to in the family as a "leaky valve," though I don't ever hear my mother say "leaky valve." To me it was wrong to speak of it like that. Like a mechanical thing or as if it were anybody's business. I would say "crude," and I mean "embarrassing," "dumb," "not right," "awful," "vulgar" (to use a word of my mother's). Rheumatic fever on my father's side wasn't quite diphtheria in my mother's family (*she* never came down with it)—outdated diseases, old as potions.

My *father's* mother remembers true stories and tells them with slow, southern glee. No describing of places or bodily acts, she quotes personages as if she's hearing their roundabout speeches for the first time so their words threaten us with wonders. My father's family, so much more frankly obligatory, had their ups and downs. These days of his death I'm aware of knowing more than I know in that quarter, an idleness in me or laziness whose nagging I will ignore, threatener that I could be. My father's family—secrecy didn't seem their way. He "helped" them.

They took a powerful interest in the letter left for me. They did not live with the same colors or smells, or at all as we lived.

My father wears his pressed trousers crisply; he *eats* with dispatch, he shifts his fork from one hand to the other, the day has darkened the room, it's Saturday lunch, and he rises and goes to the wall switch—"Let's have a little light on the subject." We're talking something over. In the letter he says to me, "... time-wasting trifles caused me to lose sight of my objective."

This letter event between me and Mom is one he won't be talking over. Was there anyone who wasn't worth talking to? *Hitler* you don't waste time with probably. (*Probably?* he says. Probably, I think. Make up your mind, one way or t'other, he says.) He got tickets to Forest Hills and we sit on a concrete level like a large step leaning forward above the grass court. Grass? but where are the bumps?, a scuffed, not-at-all lawnlike moss, we're quiet in the luxury of tennis that is a vision, no work—"effortless" is what my dad calls it. Afterward we're at a restaurant sitting on spinnable stools at the counter (it's right across the street from the steps up to the train station), but the counterman didn't act interested in bringing us the menu; he didn't actually say anything when my father asked if we could get something to eat; then my father spun around and got a menu from a booth, and he asked the man if he could find a couple of hamburgers for us. The man was scraping the grill and didn't look at us. My father shut the menu and stood up. "This fella doesn't need our business," he said. With that, we walked out, to say the least, and took the train.

His letter in my hand, I think I find his hand, his palm on my shoulder, his fingers pressing a little in on my collarbone, as we have no more of the counterman and his "behavior." I study murder cases. I investigate the earholes of a crippled bird in New Jersey and think if birds can smell. I store behind my desk an anatomy chart and know some of the muscles, know ligaments, know the hamstrings; I don't talk about it, I don't want this knowledge of mine taken note of. I know that some memories are with you and come back: and this *also* is having a good memory: which my mother and my father's mother separately tell me I have. But you think of homework and tests, a reliable *display* of memory; but it's also things to think *about*. So I just recall and recall, now when the letter in my possession with its advice *re* the future is what I should be thinking about, that I got down on the floor when I was four years old and looked up my Brooklyn grandmother's skirt in her and my step-grand-father's bedroom, and under their bed over on his side dark against the light his carpet slippers were side by side: so she said, He likes the ladies. "In retrospect," the letter says, "I am appalled by my neglect of the vistas which life has opened to me."

My father, I knew without hearing it said, was pleased with the living room of this fairly "new" apartment of ours. I, too, think it's better than other living rooms. I have not discussed such matters with him. And now he is not here to impress me. And I try to think, Is that right, what he said?

On wide winter mornings it is a seagoing living room in Brooklyn Heights, and "we" have, in addition to the bank of windows fronting on the East River end of the brilliant harbor, one single north window, "opening" north as if the builders thought they were done but then decided to knock a window out of the brick right here.

Here was the Brooklyn Bridge—too near (our fence, our majesty, our show; scale itself, but of events, how about that, Dad? But he's not here, he and I are halfway across it, hand in hand, smelling the harbor, I let go his hand, tilting our heads back to follow the mass above while he told of the men who worked on it underwater and suffered for their wages, hand in hand again); but upriver *past* the Brooklyn Bridge, the *Manhattan* Bridge (working alongside the Brooklyn but far from a copy), the envelope in my hand tells me I have daydreamed, I can know some of this half-pondering, this other bridge has the subway trains eight cars long exposed along it like workings rattling along the rails at their own speed below the cars, a bridge not noble except as all bridges are—which I think my father'd say he didn't really understand, though I haven't tried it out on him, having not *thought* it until today (or do I see that *he* said it, *he* said bridges were noble?); the Manhattan Bridge is more like streets, the jammed grimy work of the boroughs. Midtown Manhattan looked as far off as the sky, or parallel—the record height of the Empire State, the sun-mined, sky-sharpened vehicle shine of the Chrysler Building, let this be a little vague in the absence of my father. Views are overrated, *all* views, my mother's chain-smoking cousin drones, coughing, who lived for years in China. Children don't like views, she says. Don't foist views on children, they couldn't care less.

My room and my parents' room *also* offer a quiet eye on this harbor acreage. I go on about it as if I'm recommending this large apartment we might move out of, though there's no rush.

And I'm drawn to it most before I leave for school. At my own windows. From my own desk in this apartment we had moved fairly *recently* into so my room was known only to me.

And at four in the morning when a horn on the river, a clank of couplings on the docks out below my windows, *something,* would disturb me with messages, with word, and I would be awake.

Or when my father called me for dinner.

Or out in the street I'm drawn to the view in the "midst" of a hockey game standing on roller skates tall-ly bottom-heavily at rest when the leaden black-rubber puck skips over live on end and runs like a lost wheel or black-rubber gasket under a parked car on a street whose dead end *is* that view.

What was I lured *from*? (Why should I think it someone's speech or meaning?) From voices close by—soft ones, complaining ones, too. The gentlest of voices. *I* had a voice, edgier; and in my mouth smarter—or faster when I heard it played back on a thin and bendy little record I and two friends ad-libbed for a quarter in the slot of a machine at a local hotel.

I used to get up early on the new spring mornings when I was eight, nine, *seven,* keeping quiet among the created outlines of the household. Knowing my parents in bed, listening for my mother listening, I let myself out the front door and pass down the stairs of our apartment house so as not to be with the elevator man and found real freedom in the street, a street of my city, and "took a walk" *myself* along sidewalk after sidewalk, street after street, each next familiar one not quite enough. I'm un-known—out of the house—and listen for myself to the suave whine of electric power rolling the milk truck past me to the corner, where it turned, *powered* seemingly by this sound, keep-ing quiet so as not to wake people, inner and minor and smoothly recreationally simple so *I* could have driven that truck. Two dogs meet, and a third. The crazy man who normally projected his large, regular play-type false teeth almost out of his mouth at us when we were running around in the street in the afternoon I could meet now with his teeth hidden. He's snapping two fingers and looking straight ahead, he's going to work earlier than my dad, who likes to stay in bed a little longer after my mother gets up.

I told my dad about the crazy man's teeth while he was getting dressed. He laughed: "What makes you think he's crazy?" "Take my word for it," I answer and he laughs.

As a child I investigate many "matters," but I don't think my father's leaky valve is among them. I am amazed by his death; it's an action he has taken. In motion, turning, speaking, sitting down to a yellow pad, in the same voice. He has surprised me. I don't *say* this. The way I say things I pick up as I know them, or would know them.

"I didn't think you had it in you," a classmate said. I gave a speech to assembly. How easily people will say they are amazed. But maybe it happens a lot, because there is reason to believe them. If he was asking of me something in his *absence,* was it his absence itself? He wasn't *tired.* Though yes he was. Yet not of us.

You can tell from the letter that my father thought about an early death. It was in the subjects of waste and time in the letter. He expressed his hopes for me. "I have written all this because I earnestly wish you to be a better man than I am." One of his scholarships lost at the end of his first year at Harvard. A freshman alone. Really? I *felt* him alone, separated from his high school victories, his family almost. His *beliefs* painfully intact.

What got him started writing the letter, it said, was a talk he had had with a neighbor. What could they reasonably expect to leave their children? Having had that talk, my father was taking action. The letter is, I know, well *written*. It's signed in longhand, "Your affectionate father." I did not see my mother actually find the letter. Come across it; locate it. I came into the living room to that lower drawer out. I'm building backwards again. I can make my father ask what *that* means. She had the blanket chest that had belonged to her mother open one day when I was a child and she pointed out to me fitted, snug, but not squashed into a corner two packets of my father's letters before they got married, tied with blue ribbon. She pulled out one packet and I saw the beginning of one. It said, "My dearest darling," the ink endless, swift, slantingly certain with a proud unthinking rounding in some letters like the swell of a sail.

I can begin over again with the dark-eyed mother in a room of a city apartment handing the letter over. "*Building* backwards?," I can just hear my father inquire. Dark-*haired* generous mother in a spacious room handing over the letter without any flurry of mood to this not *visibly* sleepwalking son. Is any of this except the names true? No one was telling me to do anything. Not that they had to. Just be like my father, that's all *I* had to do.

How rosy on the puffed bed of the coffin's white satin lining. How of-another-material his hands, crossed. I know I'm sorry for him there as if he's missed out on things and it's not his fault. The eyelids were complete. My hazarded guess embedded far away in my sense of the occasion was that he still had a brain. Yet not that he was in any way, shape, or form asleep.

My mother's hands understood what they touched, reading a book of some composer's letters or lifting the silvery, a bit loose knob of a Dutch oven to pinch the crackly-jacketed potatoes baking on a burner; or with unthinkingly supple wrist holding with her fingertips the end of her violin bow, or with a finger of her bow hand so hastily flipping the page of her music that snatching a corner of the page it's violent, and an emergency met by a quite other personality.

One I take for granted. But I can barely see her handing me the letter. The truth is I can't. Her hand is her mind now, or my mind.

There was talk of the safe-deposit box. There was strength and fact, architecture, good metal, and a newness in the safe-deposit box, and my mother wants me to have a key to it. There it is across the river imprisoned in the barred stages of a gleaming gray basement of the Seamen's Bank, Wall Street. I have no use for a key, and am touched even more. Is the letter to be kept there, when I'm finished "with it"? I don't ask such a question, which might be a very stupid question, because there's nobody to ask. That safe-deposit box, my mother had said, was where the letter *had* been; I heard her. At the extreme bottom of one of those towering edifices, somewhat keylike. But then, no, it passed from there to a lower drawer of the desk in the living room, when she located it to give to me, a drop leaf of dark cherry.

The letter was typed. I don't see somebody else doing it; not the secretary who typed the "Market Letter" my father composed over the weekend. I'm asked to see him at a typewriter, but I don't. Though I can see him sitting up straight. I had played with typewriters seriously from an early age and from my eighth birthday had had one of my own.

He wrote on the *long* yellow pads. He wrote fast with dark-brown (-*painted*, I saw) Number 2 pencils with "Brokers Special" stamped on them in yellow gold. Why don't I recall seeing one of these without a sharp point? There are two on the large green blotter on the living-room desk. He wrote a hand so swift with that concentration of his that its absorbed regularity gained a decorative flourish. Is it, then, *not* modest? Modest maybe in a drive that looked active, useful. Reading his letter I could grasp more about time and waste than I would try to say.

The truth of "Haste makes waste" I find is in the word *makes*. My father laid down his words on paper fast. He measured them unhesitatingly, didn't he?

His hand had a flair, a looping flourish on the capitals large-scaled; I fell into it, it was an awfully smart hand, it meant what it wrote. He said, That's too fancy, when he saw my hand imitating his. I don't see him typing. I don't imagine someone else typing my letter either.

The letter was here all the time. It could wait.

The words of my father's letter come as soon as my mother hands it to me, and point at me not from his voice like a magnificent demand or thing but more from his head or his malleably gleaming scalp line above the square front of his forehead that, a few days after he dies, can still speak; and his awesomely fair ("I have to say . . ." "I'm sorry but I think you . . ." "Hey *you're* a better interrupter than *I* am" [smiling]) voice is a voice that I don't think *through* enough to come at, though later I imagine needling him. (As once, and only once, playing late in the street outside our building, and seeing him come striding home, his newspaper under his arm, I called out an unthinkable insult, showing off, that I cannot imagine myself not saying, no matter how hard I try to resay the scene.) That voice came from his eyes too, which must have fixed me more than I could help with their gray, part-colorblind *young* gaze. He sometimes gazes at me when he looks at me. *My* father had "trouble" with green and gray. It's what I can think of, as I wordlessly read his letter's words for the first time. Christian courtesy he spoke of, as if saying the words gave back some inner impress or name he could bring himself to know he had, or a conservative vividness.

I'm right: his words didn't come only from his voice. (But

from his mouth, putting intentions into shape—*mouthing* them and his "civil tongue," his excellence; civil *feelings,* it comes to me.) He's an elder of his church out there where his family *used* to live, he and his cousin Esther still go there, to sing lustily, pray that way too, it's a happiness, receive each week as if every day thoughtfully each sentence of the sermon as Dr. Arms spoke on and on. It is something of a trip out there from the Heights, it's "church," and my dad goes Wednesday evenings sometimes, too, whereas I go to Sunday School a few minutes' walk from my home, my street. On the Heights, Brooklyn Heights.

I went out to that other old gray church of big pale blocks of gray stone in another part of Brooklyn rarely. Now that he is dead, *my* not going there falls through. "*Old* church," but mine on the Heights is older. Near Henry Ward Beecher's church where Lincoln spoke. I didn't know the Sunday-School kids out at my father's church and as for my father's church friends, they spoke differently, old Bedford and Flatbush people, jovial, embarrassing for what they supposedly knew of me through knowing all about *him,* about my father. He had grown up with some of those people, they admired him, *I* knew they admired how he *spoke,* it was their faces *behind* their words greeting me jovially as his son and a fellow-*Christian* at eight or nine or ten years old and welcome because they had known my father "all his life" and more prone to refer to Jesus Christ as "Him," like my father's cousin Esther in a pink cardigan sweater. They valued and prized my father. He was better than they, I believed they thought.

"Learn to do well . . . relieve the oppressed": they believed the Bible. They said "Amen" out loud in church—"A" as in *aim,* as in ABC—which people on the Heights I felt did not. It was conversing with the minister up front, I felt. My mother said, "Ah-men" at the end of a prayer the way you *sang* "Ah-men." I heard and even *had* words, or positioned them sometimes to see they aimed, like a railroad switchman closing and opening track, though he would not have had all the time in the world. And reading and sustaining my father's letter, I have to read it and read it as a week passes—as if I've written it.

But once it was a Sunday *evening*—no radio programs that night, and my mother and father and I journeyed out to his old church to hear him give a Talk. We proceed, with a superior, pleased hopelessness, my mother and I, into a Sunday-School room. I'm looking forward to it ending, to being back home. He sat at a broad, shellacked, schoolroom-activities-type table and talked across it to everybody sitting in rows of chairs. Once, he indicated me and my mother, and he said we were an example of the "love" he had been talking about. I did not like that; I thought about it and didn't speak of it.

My father would kiss me, and kissed his stepfather—*my* step-*grand*father—and kissed his brother, my uncle, who was five years younger; and hugged, too. Though hugging and *kissing* is more with the women. "It's endless, all that kissing, coming and going, they bear down on you." It's my mother talking to *me* now. Though isn't she sort of that way, too? With *her* friends, and gaily, at the front door like an offer to dance.

With the letter in my hand that could not reach me until my father had died, I was hit with interruptions. I had a sneaking understanding that interruption was O.K., though I did it. Should I think about anything that came up to do with the letter? He wasn't here. But he was nowhere else. "Believe me, my boy, I am deeply concerned for your happiness." Was he in the letter? *If* he was, was it in the words?—or what I could make of them? I'm doing what I always do, nothing's changed, you do nothing when you're sad, you daydream, maybe you go out or you read. When will this stop happening to you?

I really treasure the letter. Delivered like that, it has an ensured force. It has been in the desk. He means those words.

My father took out not a *huge* policy or gambler's amount, like the man whose young widow my parents knew. But the

insurance company was going to lose on my father. I imagine
him learning of this. I don't dwell on money except my own,
but life insurance came to the fore. Why did I, at the age of
eleven, undergo an insurance exam? We're in a smaller apartment, then, where I walked in my sleep: right to the open
window of my bedroom, where my mother in her nightgown
and bare arms intercepted me, with cars rolling along Henry
Street six floors below. One night the insurance-company doctor
sat at my desk; my gooseneck lamp was the only light, but my
father is present. The doctor's hair was near my chest. I was
being examined *standing*. Heart, pulse, chest, blood pressure—
who knows? Could I have failed? The taking-out of that five-
thousand-dollar policy guarded me in some way. It was an adult
event that included me and singled me out. A household or
community event. Like shots at the doctor's; like the fingerprint-
ing they did on us at my Quaker school one morning. Who
knows? Is my not-knowing really letting things happen? I had
a life-insurance exam when I was eleven. Was it good of my
father? He took care of things. He looked ahead.

ii

An actual *discussion* about what to do with the letter I believe did not happen. It is my fault. Not hearing isn't so hard; for hearing is *built* almost on not-hearing. Do I recall not *noting* what was going on?

Hey, wait a minute, that's *my* letter.

I would never *quote* the letter to people. "To this day I tend to do what I find easy and slight what appears to present obstacles," the letter says.

There's a plan. A plan for the letter. But, in a way, what was being said? Not much. My grandmother looked from face to face. It was wonderful, she said, that this was being done. Pop said it was the least he could do. My delicate, slow-bodied grandmother Emmy with a reputation for being "charming" lowers her powdered, Southern, squarely delicate chin inward: she I know includes me, however subtly, her grandson and recipient of the letter, but she says softly, "Emmy has an opinion *too*." Slightly hurt is what it sounds like, is that it?, that she's kept gently out of what's going to be done with her son's letter though she's right here in her own living room. Hurt?—but maybe something else, so she's scary to me, her words come through so well, what will I do to her—Emmy, "M.E." for Mary Elizabeth—no one has consulted *her* yet, according to her: and I have almost a thought, an answer.

Pop dimples downward his dry mouth's corners where his brushy moustache stops; it is a diverted, general skeptical-pessimistic what-will-this-delightful-person-think-of-next; he'd be actually tickled, if the occasion allowed, though he can be blunt, shruggingly blunt in the middle of an occasion (and good for Pop, my *"step"*-grandfather).

Not that Emmy's going to add to the *plan*; only the mailing list. They're showing and sharing the letter, letting it be seen. We want you to read this letter he left. (My father's face hunts me down, some nearby youngness, sitting up in bed in the late afternoon looking at a couple of Christmas cards.)

Being kept just a little bit out of what's going to be done with her son's letter is equal to something, I see: to Emmy's not being *visited* or the ever-heeded prospect of not being visited, which would be a sad day if not quite final or unspeakable letdown of our expectations for the management of the world. My mind is busy. I scare myself, there's nothing left. Pop says a long "Well"...: it's his summing-up "Well" (pronounced "Whale") signaling the "that's all there is to it" facts of the matter: "Well ... more people should see this." Which sounds (to my ear) equal to his "I've always said."

I look down on him but then I imagine him on the South American run, he's heaving a line to a dark man on the dock who hauls it, the great loop of the bight, to a bollard and works it over it; yet Pop was actually a passenger, but I can believe *he* saw this happening, too.

Upon which, he pounds the arm of his wing chair with his hand that holds my father's letter. I watch it, God curse me that's what I'm doing. Many times unfolded and refolded, it was folded when my mother gave it to him and he has folded it again. He read it last week and gave it back—to me—and I think has read it now again, certainly has looked and looked at it. I want to not kill or torture or even humble him but yell him or flood him away, but yes, humble him, *tell* him something that has not been told, hit him with something I can almost grasp, like an obstacle, and a thought comes into me and, "to say the least," I'm not ready for it (which is *another* thought), and I better believe my father telling me how "Dad" played tennis with him in the park.

This wiry countryman who works in a printing shop?—playing on a white-lined tennis court?—and the primitive un-reality of tennis in 1913 or '14? I, who play tennis, do not imagine it of this man I understood was from the towns and hidden, loon-occupied lakes of Maine who works, who does fine work, in a job-printing shop and returns with Emmy for a month's fishing to Maine in the summertime, wears olive-green rough wool sportsman's breeches, takes me cut by cut through the gutting and cleaning of white perch we caught, a whole school of them, at dawn.

"Boy" (he calls me) "your father was some kind of man." What have I done? Emmy says, "He *cer*tainly *was,*" with a slow, quavery fierceness loyal in its historical sweep even to me I can feel so that again I am maybe behind-hand or wanting. Have I been found wanting, been caught red-handed?

"Yes," from my mother, her body separate in a soft brown-and-gray suit in this room that isn't at all hers, her voice distinctly husky, "he certainly *was,*" the subtle ascent of tone stressing in seeming discovery what kept *her beyond* "the family" yet just barely within this general agreement. My great-aunt Edna says blessedly, even truly, her voice cracking, "He knew how to laugh." And at this pace I find time to wonder what there *is* to know in order to laugh, and I know I don't know how to think of this letter he left me or am somewhat betrayed into *not* thinking.

And Esther, her daughter, with this objectivity I like or feel promoted by, but haven't figured out except it seems in her Christianity, her "religion," adds in tacit memory, "He had a nice way of joking." There is broken-voiced sighing that doesn't quite make it to modest laughter from the women, except my mother, who smiles with the effort of hearing exactly what is theirs to share, but my mother has not audibly sighed, and when it is over, Aunt Edna and then her daughter give the silence one more little musical or digestive sound, which is a little like one or two brief "units" of a small baby's crying only it's cheerful, it "says" that the reason we laughed is with us still in spirit; it is also Southern, because, while *Emmy* never "does it," her other sister, my great-aunt Callie and *her* maiden daughter in their apartment or here, do "the same thing," in *unison* or one after the other.

These are still early days of my father's death, it isn't "where has the time gone" but where *can* it go, and this tells upon the *importance* of his letter and why and how it is to be "dis*posed* of " (I might put it) as the letter evidently *is* going to be disposed of. I might be looking out at the vista of the harbor, or stupidly sleuthing just where the letter was when. Pop shipped down the coast of South America once and came back and married Emmy, I know.

As if I'm in another room and I divine that I am not alone, I recall OKing or silently not OKing what is happening to the letter.

I don't hear myself being asked—that is, what I *think*; but I was not left out by the others. It seems a common decision. If a "decision" at all.

I couldn't figure how to make the needed sounds—if only to point out what was "open to us," and think first what that was. I couldn't keep it in my desk; or it could be glassed-in in a box like a document in museums my father to tell the truth took me to. Or it could be memorized by everyone and then thrown away or buried secretly. There was little *for* me to say, apart from starting to speak without knowing what I would say. I did not "stop" to think of the things I *could* have said to those people. *Was* I in on this group deed? It was his gift. Who was the group anyway? Who was "competent to handle" whose affairs? The letter is handled, it is not quoted.

I speak of his family, "the" family. On my grandmother's lips, "family" means that she has a steady aim, for example my father making a special trip out to see her on a night when he needs some encouragement to do so. My mother sees how it worked and will tell me, but not how it came down to the word use. I'm in high school. I have seen *these* things a long time, as early as the age of nine or ten, having felt them earlier, but don't quite voice them to myself until now when the letter is being discussed in "the family's" living room. I don't believe the physical impulse to value others is generally missing. I believe it's there, but I get horrifically, certainly uncomprehendingly mad.

Esther uses "family" to mean foibles, the endearingly reliable kind. My uncle, he said "family" to mean what his mother wanted, very humorous in his raised eyebrows and with his laugh that I guess I haven't been laughing along with—it's not *silly* laughter. It's I think why my mother says a thing or two about him. I am using this word. I am not using this word "family" myself much. I sounded the word in my mind. As if to an audience who can be pleased. Or as if something would happen. Like my mother some of the time calling Emmy "Mother"—as Emmy had asked to be called from the beginning. From the honeymoon on; in a letter dispatched to my father in Bermuda, I'm told. My mother *had* a mother; or my mother's grown out of having a father and mother, but even after that grand, long-skirted person down in New Jersey died, my mother still *had* had a mother.

"The family" here means four persons, four members of my father's "immediate" family (on his "side"); through them I hold to the tedium and sometime quiet of the named streets, the markets, the streetcar they call "the car." I give "the family" credit in the midst of a discussion of what will be done with my father's letter: they make me think of ancient Brooklyn, and I absorb it also from my distance of downtown "advantages." "To this day I tend to do what I find easy and slight what appears to present obstacles," my letter says. Already, if I bypass the names of these folk with the fullness or feelable shorthand which the names could have, the possibilities of meaningless accounting and explaining bump into place. I hear myself tell (tell who?) that the subway ride further into Brooklyn was longer both ways, and taxis down in the secluded streets of the Heights were mysteriously absent. Pop is pounding his fist on the arm of his chair and my father's letter rustles as it lifts and falls. They sat in their armchairs with crocheted antimacassars, my father's family. They liked visits.

It is not accurate, not right to say I see my father making that trip alone: in the dark or the cold or on a Sunday: to see his mother: I mean, *alone* and to see *her* more than anyone *else*. Yet I do see that. And because I'm with him sometimes.

To see also "Dad," his stepfather, or "Pop." (Which means I have a step-*grand*father.) And to see my great-aunt, more gaunt-seeming than fragile, tall, one of my grandmother's *two* widowed sisters, the one who lives there, Edna, they chuckle together. (I could change everything except the names.)

And to see, in the sense that she was more than visible, my great-aunt's daughter, my father's cousin Esther, three years younger than my father, who sleeps in the same room with her mother.

My father can't come and see them anymore. He's dead.

Pop's job, Esther's job become interesting all of a sudden. The jobs move upon my father's letter. Pop's job because he is a printer, I've been to his shop three times, once years ago he

lost his job and became a printer. Why *Esther's* job? They like
their jobs. They are the breadwinners. The "family" is like one
person alone—or unit, I see—after my father's death.

My great-aunt Edna spoke least and therefore has to have
been fourth of the four in the earlier days of my childhood
except that she is a *mother,* and *Emmy's sister* and so was third,
and her daughter was fourth at that time. They were a group I
did not see dispersed or, like myself, wandering over the streets
of the borough and the city.

In the letter, my father credited his Christian upbringing.
He expressed gratitude for the love "Mother and Dad" had given
him when he was at Boys High doing six hours' homework a
night. The school's name doesn't sound like "boys" to me.

My mother has said, "He was so poor." My father is ten
when his real father dies, a lawyer, this mystery man. As for me,
I saw Emmy and Pop walk Pop to the front door in one moving
hug step step step step, a walk-dance. I had not seen any other
people do that. I didn't speak of it. He was off to work: what
was I doing? Staying. There is no school for me apparently that
day unless it's one of those Saturdays he went to Manhattan to
his shop and I spent Friday night with them winning at Casino;
he *has* to work that Saturday. It was funny for them, me as
audience for that moving hug. I was just seeing what they *always*
did, I knew.

He was "tickled" by her, even "had fun." That much I knew,
in the sense that I know I knew at eight years old or nine or
earlier that that walk-dancing hug, which wasn't anything I was
proud of or would tell my friends, was not something I had seen
except here. I did not speak to my mother about it, and so, in
my observation of my grandmother in her bathrobe and my
step-grandfather in this walk-step to the door, knowing they
didn't do it just for me, a cozy mystery or odd little party hovered
in these two.

And in the midst of the discussion of what was to be done with the letter, I pondered this charm—of the two of them or of her. Because of my mother and her insights (plus in me a pinprick of not taking sides, a bit of neutral, warranted meanness). In those earlier times, I was a child and I put down on top of that dance-hug a later *map* or some very loose-woven article of clothing. It's more words than rugs, room thresholds, the sound of their moving from rug to floor, more than floor plan and colors; but it's the coast, and a phrase, "from Maine to Georgia": for at the age of five or six or seven *I* knew this white-haired lady to have a Southern Accent, and my step-grandfather I knew to be from the pine woods and lakes of Maine, the sinews, the isolated muscles and awful little cords of his resistant body: as resistant to what I could not quite try to want from him as he was able to prize and enjoy me, like not nipping my finger when I'm messing around with his brush-harsh moustache and he's snapping, snapping, really too much like an animal, so I'm surprised when he laughs at the end.

The letter from my father was soon shown to my father's family. Shown as soon as I got it, I think. (Though my *uncle* and I are shaking hands and it's our own apartment where I give the letter to *him* to read, for its certain effect on him.) Yet I may have been recklessly shy, and my mother would have told my grandmother of the letter on the phone, whatever she felt when she hung up. "The family" knew of it by telephone, because they already knew of it when they were given it to read. They *could* not see it before it passed from my hand to theirs. By way of my mother. But from my inside jacket pocket to their living room. No more would I say what was originally in the envelope for me. And was not asked.

My step-grandfather said the letter was very well-written. My grandmother said that my father had a wonderful mind. My step-grandfather's literalness and quickness could all but take something from you, but why let him?—but with *hesitant* authority here, with love for my mother, the young widow, his absolute grief unspeaking until the *letter* was to be spoken of.

Experience was the best teacher, according to his grade-school copybook. Well, it was *his* experience he was talking about. My father only a couple of years ago helped him buy the house in Maine, which was a way of *every*one going there in the summer. Danvers, Massachusetts, was really where he was from, my mother said; he'd spent *time* in Maine—when he was a child. My mother said it was very good of my father. The first summer they spent two weeks there. I was at camp and my mother rather vividly, yet like advice, told me that my grandmother would be heard calling my father, asking him where he was—upstairs, downstairs, on the porch, in the parlor. Not like a game. It drove him nuts. He was reading, reading in the country.

He was heard to say more than once that when he had brought home a report card with five A's and a C, Pop his *step*father had asked what this C was doing here. Did my father speak of this like a Marine surviving boot camp or not? My father would have been looking ahead always, ahead beyond the gray stone of Boys High, the six courses, the Latin and French, solid geometry, chemistry, the famous teachers. But also looking *into* that powerful life, which in its restricted arduousness must have rewarded him or sufficed, even to making the ultimate scholarships to Harvard that he achieved harder to live with. His real father's death widowed his mother in her early thirties, turned her out of her basic life. Dumped her south, for a moment, a few months. But she just went home to another place she was familiar with—town in Georgia—until she came back to Brooklyn. Rented another house and took in roomers. The cooking was very very good, "too good," my father said, and this young man ("from Maine" as I saw him) who worked for the Underwood Typewriter Company and had been to South

America to extend their trade in that part of the world rented a room from her.

And so he fell in love with my grandmother: I could see that still. He took on the two sons. So he did not have his own. In age, he was about halfway between my grandmother and my father. He was much loved by them and my father helped him out later on. My grandmother and her new husband—but I think of her as her *name* and as "my father's mother"—moved and moved again, to Halsey Street, names unchanged, then to New York Avenue in the Bedford-Stuyvesant section of Brooklyn; and with her came her younger sister and that woman's daughter. My grandmother was *used* to living with her relatives. Too much so, my mother felt. And to Brooklyn came also her older sister, also widowed young, and *her* daughter. But they lived in Flatbush, though not far away. This man "from Maine"—"Pop," as he was called—got laid off by Underwood and went to work as a job printer and journeyed to Manhattan on the subway for four decades looking up at the advertising spaces at the edge of the ceiling. They took a cruise once and he won all the deck-tennis matches and some other events.

The room's heat rises through my head, can't get out. Where they live now, discussing my father's letter. Yet there was no discussion. The ladies in their white cardigan sweaters need the steam heat. Not my mother. Not me. She is lovely to them. She is sweet in her smile, in her agreeing. There is a proposal— "plan" sounds good—to take my father's letter and print it up and send it to friends of the family. It is put to my mother and me, but it has come as a thought from my mother, not today, somehow previously, but not a distinct thought. The action would have a worthwhile promptness, it's only about three weeks since my father's passing. My mother said to my step-grandfather that this was a fine thing to do with the letter. She and I, God knows, were together. The discussion was between her and Pop. It had the future in it, and since it was partly my letter it was sort of my future, so it had love in it, yet it had nothing in it for me, the letter as a *subject* for their discussion. Other things that could have been done with the letter were not discussed, though I would not have been able to imagine what they were unless someone had thrown that potentially *entertaining* question to me.

I make a swift list of how I thought of the letter in their presence: *silence, spelling, precious, lacrosse, money, empty, unreadiness, banana smell, what-do-we-do-now?-nobody-really-knows, waiting, white paper, I'm here today, open casket, churchgoing, amount to much.*

But the two who talked, or talked most, and in taking for granted like history the printing of the letter as being implied by the letter more or less took the lead—namely, my step-grandfather and my mother—were, respectively, an atheist who seldom or never voiced his irritation with this Jesus guesswork; and a musical Christian. "Atheist," the word is blunt, I almost must say more, but he said life was simple, and he *is* blunt, though he couldn't be an atheist just because he didn't go to church, could he? The phrase for "her," my mother, is somebody else's, my mother plays in church occasionally (so small an instrument, that violin, smaller still to hold, so great as a seeming silencer of the organ, so telling a sound under that roof of my church) and when sitting in a cushioned pew downstairs and standing with the congregation she particularly liked singing the hymns in parts, and if she didn't relax into the prayers—but like me had her eyes open though in her case maybe squintingly—she might have been whimsically resting. We are listening to people shuffle and cough around us and early American pew backs creaking, then the organ resumes the stately tale of the Handel music, or its *thinking,* and the slow, firm contralto creates resolution and firmness, "I know that my Redeemer liveth," like love outside me it seems, and my mother and I, not at all atheistically, look at—or see—each other for just a second or two, it's nothing to do with God's (as our minister said) intervention into human history, much less with thinking things through, much more with the melody and its hope of agreeing.

Three or four rooms crucial to me ease apart and I keep coming away. The rooms are in two apartments but they run together into one. Our apartment; and "the family's" elsewhere in Brooklyn.

But the one elsewhere in Brooklyn *itself* spreads apart, time spreads it, into two: the "railroad"-halled second-floor walkup in what became a "changing neighborhood" (with on the floor in the public hall downstairs cold, sooty-white bathroom tile designed in little black-outlined diamonds and carpeting on the stairs we walked up to the second floor to see them and where Pop to avoid disturbing Emmy when the doctor was there when she was critically ill with a heart attack she survived as I felt sure she would, sat crying on one of those carpeted stairs telling my father her condition in every detail, his voice softly breaking *a-hanh a-hanh a-hanh* while I thought of what smell, the not-good smell, the stairs had, like cooking but without the roasty heat or boiling things); and then the *third*-floor apartment near the park in the elevator building where they're living only about a year now at the time of my father's removal—but not as if they would need my father's help to go on here.

Pop's plan was to print up the letter in a hundred copies and send them to friends of the family. *Many* people would be impressed by the letter, or touched: *I* knew that. They would read it through, but I did not know, or really think, what they would say, they'd nod their heads or shake their heads, but I am imagining the *life* of each of them with the letter in it and can't spell that out to myself. It was a little show-offy, after all, sending it out.

Pop wanted to show us the printing job as soon as it was done. He phoned my mother one day to tell us. Then Emmy phoned and we went out there to dinner. "There it is. I think it came out pretty well," Pop said. What if he had said, "Here it is"? A small point. Trivial. It was a present to my father.

My grandmother said that it was a wonderful letter, and that she was happy it would be read by "others." Hers is some confiding method of slow Southern explaining that was a passing of the time of day. She cried easily yet it was audible only in the words she was speaking *while* she cried, she did not look away when she cried, she looked still more closely at you, looked you *over*, and all too tenderly. They're sentimental, the women of my father's family, my mother says. This must be so. My grandmother's humor was to remind me two weeks in advance of her birthday. I accept the "sentimentality" label as what *we* thought of "them."

At Christmas dinner, which *this* Christmas because my father wasn't feeling "up to snuff" we didn't have with them, the snuffling at two or three "places" around the table as a Christian grace found its nostalgic range before seeking its conclusion was mentioned later by my mother but was less of a thing to *me* than Pop's renewed wielding of the carving knife as if he had been wielding it in his *mind* all through grace. This skill of his is spoken of in the family, so it is waiting for these moments, his plain readiness, when at last the bird is ready for *him,* skill he takes for granted like the for-the-moment-uncommunicative star athlete just before the event, whose self-importance under the eyes of the crowd is legitimate and even called for; though not taken for granted by me, in me it went *with* another exercise, mine, and slightly terrible in *my* accuracy *watching* him do it: though as far as his *display* of skill went, that was his point, instructively sharing what he anatomically knew. Is it a bit of shame at this accurate technical attention of mine that gets me through the grace or "thinking" that when he's actually eating he doesn't switch his fork from his left hand to his right but brings the food to his mouth with his fork held as he might hold it when cutting with the knife in his right hand, whereas my mother and father switch hands?

I call my father's mother by her first name. She'll sit down in her armchair in the "parlor" and ask, "What's the news?" as if we lived in a town like my other grandmother in New Jersey. Words were required, and for a purpose, but any old chitchat would do, but if I wanted I could choose anything, and only in this sense "making up" what I was to tell her. But now at fifteen but especially with my father's death no longer a lever at least *waiting* to be used—this request to be told the news supported my perfect importance, entertaining not just her but her sister Edna and Edna's middle-aged daughter, Esther, and others, with pretty tepid reports in really another tongue of school and neighborhood which made them for some reason marvel, or shake their heads.

It stayed with them, their amusement, possibly my words. I knew I had not done anything, though, and felt I did not want to be there; I would have liked to be told something surprising at length. After the hearty laughter there comes (for me with the suspense of a second's silence or breath) that odd subsiding after-laugh, a communication between themselves more like words concurring. The passing scene, people my grandmother didn't know. Because of this, since I always from an early age saw her as a widow, though she had remarried my step-grandfather—maybe a model widow because she had managed—but a woman in need, I see her widowhood as an immobile waiting. To receive something. News. People. And yet within the home she moved. I see her as a widow who sees me as what has been going on "outside," in a better sphere. While I guess and almost grasp my not seeing that its betterness was only, for her, a pleasant fact.

My great-aunt Edna, with her modestly accelerated beginnings followed by genuine utterance, said that my father's letter *reminded* her of him, he had a way with words, why, reading his letter he might just be still here with us. Her closeness to her daughter there in that household makes her seem not a widow. This daughter, my father's cousin Esther, shared the other bedroom with her in that apartment, shared much with her mother. Esther is around forty-two, around my mother's age, at this awful and religious time of my father dying. Anyone may imagine her grief, which was not ignorance.

She read the letter the evening I first brought my copy, and she reread it, narrowing her eyes here and there as if to understand better, her very dark eyebrows with gray hairs in them— she was *thinking* with a look of objectivity I thought I trusted, I liked it *and* her, or was attracted and diverted by it. She says I am fortunate to have had such a father, and I feel like saying, "I still have him," knowing also that I think he might be alive in another continent. Whatever other remarks mean, hers means she has been fortunate to grow up in the same household with him, and when, in that warm room, she then looked up into my eyes, a thinking humbleness in her manner added belief to the slight hone of possibility that *he* was fortunate to have *me*. How does she do that? There's the flicker of amorphous esteem it locates in me as if its start was in me.

It was her methodical, respectful *re*reading. This made the letter seem mine, that she was being given the privilege of reading. I knew, going home, that I was not myself at this time, and I said to a girl I knew that I thought I had gone to sleep, those words kept coming to me.

This actual, unmessage-like thing left to me, I was letting it be thought of by others *or* letting it be *not* thought of by others. When you competed, was it *for* some*thing* or *against* some*one*? I wasn't thinking about the letter in my father's thorough way. I felt this would be ungenerous.

When I go to college a year and a half later, I start to think (though without wishing to understand or grasp) that the letter might be "mine."

At my father's death I "get" it and so I understand that it is mine. I didn't think of it as changing. Or didn't think at all about it in the sense of trying to. The reactions to the letter in the family hollowed the true volume my father could no longer occupy even if he tried like a liquid or other substance. And did so with a readiness that might be as different as the death itself.

The deed—my step-grandfather's deed—grew murky, spread, yet was a nice piece of printing; a new oddity, a new excellence, like the death—but an intermittent irritation, *un*like the death—the death stays from this day to the next, alien, comprehensive, a power not previously here, not at all ugly or at war, possibly grand.

I made of this soon after the dissemination of my father's letter what no one around me, to my knowledge, made of it. "Natural," "good," "yes," "fine," were words used for this hopeful, living, family and general "action taken" on my father's letter. He had written it after all.

I had no carbon of it.

It was to be handsomely printed by my step-grandfather, and just at a time when I felt that that relation *step*-grandfather was not the regular thing—an inheritance, an oddity, but not interesting; not quite normal, but true. I thought I could stand all things. Anything except being dismembered by an atrocious prison torturer—discussed with guys at school, one of whom was going to be a lawyer, his father was one. "Handsomely printed," the letter bore the title "Letter from [and my father's name, his initials and last name] to his son": just like that. I could like its accuracy. The lawyer-to-be classmate wrote a letter to me a couple of days after my father died—that soon—saying he was very sorry to hear the news. It was handwritten. He was a mine of information as a rule.

As for my father's letter, I don't take up with my mother how we feel about a whole lot of people reading it; I think she with some helpless depth will dismiss such effortful efforts devoted to issues made slight or awkward by events (by days) of powerful, best wordless feeling. I might have taken it up with her because I did almost take up with her why after all she *shouldn't* have her way and leave the casket closed at the funeral home, but she had already consented without a complaint, which was almost what she was complaining to me about. My grandmother had been feeling poorly that week he died, that wearying, hour-by-hour yet swift week he was in the hospital; and she hadn't had a visit with him, yet my mother was right that this wasn't why Emmy said it would mean so much to her to have the casket open. To "see" him—to dwell upon person or man through the so-near so-far mannequin glamour he could be seen as—though she could not reach him now by telephone.

Four weeks later I am official in my step-grandfather's title for the letter: it seemed O.K.

One hundred copies were going out. I then feel it's made for those people. Stagefright proud, I think of them reading it.

My mother is on her bed in her dressing gown sitting up and she's reading the letter. I'm only in the doorway. Stockings are draped on my father's bed. She purses her lips at me complexly, not a kiss or reproof but a little "off," and holds the letter up in one hand and shakes it at me. As if she is not mainly reading it but waiting for me—to say something, do something.

My parents sent a lot of Christmas cards. *He* was reading a couple of cards sitting up in his bed one afternoon before Christmas. He would go to the office but he said he was feeling bushed. I would come into the bedroom and sit down on the other bed.

One card is from a close friend of my parents, a lawyer who was at Oxford, who composed a sonnet every Christmastime and had it printed up and sent out. My father could find interesting things in his friend's Christmas sonnet, reads it aloud in good humor, I recall only the spirit of those annual poems and that the Prince of Peace wound up the victor in the final lines; yet no, I recall words.

He was much loved. The letter my father had left for me was words. I saw this soon after I received it, yet saw it gradually. I read the sentence about how "Dad and Mother" had impressed on him always that they would not be able to send him to college and he would have to earn scholarships in order to go. (There was nothing in the letter about his real father, who had been "doing well" when he died.)

I have read individual words like "Felix," the first name of his friend he had the talk with one evening that inspired the letter. Or I neglected the letter, forgot it. Went to school. Or coming home from the subway had an exchange, a shuffling, near-shoving near-fight with two public school kids one afternoon.

I know who gets copies on our side, but many on the "family"'s side were friends of my grandparents whom my mother really didn't know. My step-grandfather and my grandmother were content and proud. They would not have seen that they got what they wanted. Pop reported what the family of his boss had said, and cited his boss's pet passage:

> I know that my crowning failing is a tendency to hope
> that a wished-for result will come about by itself, with
> little or no aid from me or effort on my part.

My grandmother talked over the phone about the letter to her other sister, also a genteelly non-expatriated refugee from Georgia, who lived in Flatbush with *her* daughter. They were tiny women in very high heels, and this other great-aunt was more comfortable with her firm will than even my grandmother and wore tiny stylish veiled hats and "had a fall" down the steps of the subway station or *up* the steps of the trolley maybe once a year. My grandmother needs her sisters nearby. My great-aunt Callie has a person-to-person, slightly taken-for-grantedly serious way of talking and flirting with me from the time I'm quite little that has the pleasing effect of sending me on my way, even when called "Sugar," establishing me as someone honorably separate from her, scintillatingly so.

She asked me once what *I* thought of the letter. It was a polite question, but she wanted to know. It is kind of smart of her, "intelligent," to do that. I remember from day to day, because I do not remember anyone else asking.

I almost immediately find myself doing things that my father would—or could—have known of, whether I discussed them with him or not. I don't get the chance to keep things from him now or be moody that he felt this way or that about me. But then I *do*—I see I do, but I don't have to try, unless he is God.

In its new copies the letter seemed to belong to my mother. Or it was near her a lot. It was like her folded stationery where you opened to the next page and it was really page 3 facing you though in Pop's printing page 2 had not been wasted. It was just a job of printing, and a handsome one. But no, the letter never belonged to her. Yet she gave something more than her approval to its being printed up.

One man who naturally received a copy—his wife *and* he got one—had come to the apartment the day after my father died. He was outrageously formal as I could tell, though I heard it often; elaborate of manner, a man of sincerely measured cordiality. As if he might be getting ready to carve, or as if you were somebody. My father understood him, I knew. This man had studied at Oxford and was called "Doctor" before his name; he was the Christmas sonnet writer; he had five or six old pistols in working order mounted on a wall of his living room near a window. He was a lawyer, he went to Grace Church, he had a moustache with waxed ends. He on occasion punished his son, I recall it as being talked about, an old-fashioned beating—only public in some *feeling* of my memory; and he was proud of his son, I mean *specific* in reporting what his son did, his life of action and regulations, and he kissed his son, who was hardy, generally under control, seemingly better at talking than I (though, granted, older), and proprietor (backed by his father yet subtly not quite *with* his father, who made requests but as if to the executive engineer) of a giant landscaped model-train system in the great attic of their house. This father-man was well-informed to an extreme, and he and my father mingled their learning, were fond of each other. He seems too different from my father, doesn't he? He mixes Manhattans so strong he seems not to understand something, they seem to my amused parents a mistake; like my father he would address a subject either with a sprightly fact or with a hushed, concerted concern as for an emergency.

He was, perhaps, more than formal, and he was very glad to see you. I take his coat in the foyer, my mother is in the living room at the far end of the hall with the others. I take his coat. The hall closet is full. This man detains me like an equal (yet only in my sense, my sudden protectively important, more than vital, sense of my relation to my mother). And in his in a way same old frowning concern I find—I *find*—*not* the same thing but an expression *of* it that is shock. Part of him has gone away with my father, I swear. My time sense is either confused or very powerful. The letter in the living-room desk has not been found by my mother yet.

He is saying to me, he's saying to me, that he "loved" my father very much, and if I ever need him to talk to, or for any *other* reason, he would be proud to be a father to me.

I did not think of what to say. I thanked him, with thanks and not strangeness in my heart and a few blind words. I am good. I have let him go down the hall to the living room, where his wife has preceded him. What *I* do is, I turn and go into the guest room to be overcome. To cry, leaning against the wall. This visit—that man—whose formalness strikes you rather hard as an act he carries through with a grammatical true-to-form-ness, it's politely fearsome, something of him *will* love you and *he* does, and yet his so familiar tact—it is grief, his grief, and I have to admit, or see, he is sentimental, in his waxed moustache and his predicted *ways*. I love him for a time, he doesn't see himself from anywhere but inside, he has found himself ready in manner and attention to put his grief into action. In my tears in the guest room I know I won't *steadily* feel this, but do now knowingly. Does he not see himself at *all*? Advice he has offered me: and I already, a day after my father's death, in my importance here might ask them anything—my parents' men friends—it would be easy.

His word "proud" valued me, like an associate. I think that I am overwhelmed: not unhappily; more like a personage employed. I am doing a lot. I am much more than stricken, and I'm less. I don't need to plan.

Later on today, I think that this man has lost a friend who heard him, and he was alone, left like me, a *wildly* formal man, bereaved. Why did my father like all that? It doesn't matter, I see. Gertie was in the kitchen helping out. She had changed her clothes in the maid's room.

The letter will answer all those sonnets.

All that was *not* in the letter comes near. A large, fine living room: it opened at one end into a dining room and along the harbor side into a music room. Why yes, I come to feel that some of these things *aren't* in the letter.

There are three bedrooms—the guest room all by itself at the end of the long hall, and off this hall on one side a "maid's room" with its own dark bath, and on the other the entrance to the kitchen right by the foyer and the front door.

The letter was a thing, never mind the contents. It was other than a "thing" once it was dispatched and dispersed into Brooklyn, Manhattan, Connecticut, Maine, and to my mother's brother and younger sister in New Jersey and to Maryland and to my mother's older sister in Texas and to Cleveland to one of many business friends, and to a woman living in Nevada who's a one-time relative by marriage, didn't want any children, remarried a cowboy, bought two ranches, and came East once a year, interestingly beautiful and resolutely peaceful in her very sharp intelligent and ivory temperament if not her new religion called Mental Science given to wiping off her silver with her napkin at our place or out. She loved my father.

He was much loved. The words are true. *In Wall Street.* By associates and clients. A once-well-to-do, possibly dissolute class-mate borrowed money from him after graduation and never paid him back. It was morally beneath contempt, I understood, yet I would like to know much more about that man. I would be surprised to hear that that man was on the letter list. My mother got in touch with that man once, to collect the money after all that time, and I remembered his name because we never heard from him. And because he was nicknamed "Baron" in college—yet have I proof this wasn't his Christian name? I ask this of my mother, who frowns and smiles and her face transfers its look to her shoulders or chest in a motion so obvious to me, so terribly inadequate and stubbornly subtle or hurt that I can't bear it, and am too poor; hers is a bewildering shrug too fine almost to perceive in her upper body, her short-sleeved sweater: "What's it matter?" she says, and I can't tell her. I know what my parents said, and I could grasp more, it doesn't trouble me where it exists possibly an opposite to what I think if not always say. It's O.K. to keep quiet, but maddening and really sort of secure.

I myself do not send out any copies. I leave this chore to others. The man who was once at Oxford praised the reference to Churchill: "When his direst predictions materialized, his country turned to him, recognizing the need for a man who was not easily discouraged and whose determination knew no bounds." My mother has sent a few copies to people I know better than she. My minister's son I know *saw* the letter, a friend who could be my closer friend if I were wiser—I know this. And he showed it to a girl who had known of my father's death before I did.

We had all been having a party in the social rooms at the church the Friday night my father died. When my uncle came to get me, *she* learned of his presence downstairs and, like my own private family, went down and met him. Then she came upstairs to get me, where I was in love with a dark-haired girl, and had put the hospital windows and hard shining floors and my father's bed out of my mind for a few hours though I had been putting the cellophane-like oxygen tent (its separating fragility and its camping-equipment look) and my father's preoccupation with breathing half out of my mind all week, his smile to me, his wordlessness, his hard-working smiling wordlessness.

My uncle came to the church, and my friend, the girl who came back upstairs to get me, knew what I did not know yet from his mouth, his voice, his neck, the angle of his imperceptible bow toward me, I was not willing that that awful report be given me. My uncle is within the church building this Friday night—the rear part that houses the offices and Sunday School and the social rooms, and only adjoins the dark church. I went downstairs to where he was waiting.

I know that my father is dead before my uncle takes a step toward me and says my name—or practically dead. But I know that my father is still *some*where. My uncle, therefore, is only my uncle coming, even unexpectedly, to "get" me. And my father is in the hospital and couldn't be here. "And so" my uncle is not coming *instead* of my father. My uncle was not supposed to be there. He has his car.

He takes my arm. He walks differently. During the walking, it is to me that this has happened. They didn't call me to the hospital.

From the dark back seat as I got in the front, my mother said, "It's too bad," as if she were saying also, "isn't it?"; and I

held the words between us for a second and settled in the front
seat to stare heavy and ignorant and half-alive through the wind-
shield at the street lights. I must have nodded to her. Now all
three of us in the car know we know. My uncle has called "the
family" from the hospital. My uncle's nose, his subdued pleasure
in driving: I am hardly hearing him, what he is saying, how
my father's temperature went up to a hundred and seven and
they gave him a shot of adrenalin. It passes by my eyes that my
uncle is like me, we might just chat. We *might*. My uncle knows
you're there in the other seat. My uncle is a good son. He takes
it more lightly. I think he eloped once, so it would have been
impossible for his mother to write *him* on his honeymoon. My
father will sit down with him, he worries about him. He loves
his brother. I don't know what is going to happen when we get
home. It's better in the car, the streets, the street lamps. My
father is dead this evening. I don't have to do anything. My
father has been away in the hospital for a week. I see the inside
of the hall closet.

One of the things I thought about the letter from my father
when my mother found it and gave it to me and I took it away
to my room and "had" it for a time, was: What *could* you really
say about it? One of the great discussers: had he closed the
subject?

My mother did not ask. And our relative silences agreed the
letter was my father's "fine" (more than *a* father's) "fine," *good*
letter. A "loving father" is what we could have said if we had
tried to say it to each other. And while the letter stressed, if only
for a sentence or two, how he hadn't worked hard enough at
Harvard (though to me he made it sound practically the opposite—and it wasn't "about how" at all, it only said that) and,
looking back now, he regretted not "making more" of himself—
sacred words but he is my father, what "more" would he have
made?—I half-grasp now but don't explain it to myself that his
summing-up of college on Washington's Birthday in 1943 when

he wrote the letter is *prophetic* in being *remembered*. My uncle acted dumbfounded. I enjoyed his seeing it. He shook his head and looked up at me. He was holding the letter in both hands and he let go with one hand but kept that hand right next to the letter, he looked back down at the letter. For a while I figured I would do as well as I could. Then he was able to talk again, and started talking.

My uncle has really needed my father. My uncle used to drive a red Buick touring convertible with a full back seat. He is a good three inches taller than my father. I know all about him. He has done things for me, has taken me places. He thinks I'm smart. With him I am.

My uncle does not say things that surprise me.

He hands back the letter.

"I don't know what I'll do without him," he says as if in courtesy to me when he felt like saying nothing. A man who talked a lot. He has a long, long laugh, and I know he should cut it short sometimes.

He was not especially excited about spreading the letter around. I know this.

I would not have felt able to go to the funeral home to look at caskets without him. You have to buy one; people buy them; I love him. Mother and uncle and I pay a visit to the funeral home to pick out a casket for my father, and I put the word "coffin" aside. The caskets are displayed stacked in twos, their satin looks like you would have to get dead in a hurry if you touch it; they are surprisingly huge—or their length turns the showroom into an alcove.

No, but first we passed from the carpets of the reception area in another part of the great compartmented building and into a dark theater really with banks of seats curving a little at the edges. I'm fascinated, it's like the World's Fair, but the suspense grips me. This place was empty and dark except for a bright light of an unusual clear directness up front. There was a woman in the casket up there, its satin a silver white around her and against her. It all gave *back* light to the light. She was powdered and emphatic, her hair very done and bluish. She was in a blue gown as if to receive people. She was fighting it all off, no hands, inwardly without looking. I stared as we walked across the back of the chapel, and my seeing her steadily out of the corner of my eye felt like my *mother* had *not* noticed. I'm a little bit outraged. Scared for what was happening to my father somewhere near us. She *was* all alone, though dead.

I grasp that there's another way to see all this. And that I am *doing* what I am doing. My father no longer knew me. A force in me struggled to not-understand. Some possibly pure movement occurred there, I could not observe it. I thought I was lost, about to be killed, I guess.

I put down in a diary a picture of that lady lying all made up ready for the service, though what kind of service could you have in a place like that, a place of business? Being alone just was not part of it. She was separately still. She was dead. But I don't say she wasn't personal. My mother's arm held my hand close to her, the back of my hand was against the side of one of her breasts and my fingers curl firmly over her arm.

But in the showroom adjoining the chapel I got that dead woman into my head. The dead woman was so much *older* than my dad. Yet she was not as old-looking as my *grand*mother; or she had an *active* look. My uncle deferred to my mother; he seemed to be as knowing as the funeral man while we looked at caskets. It was only between *two* caskets.

My father was afraid my uncle would lose his arm when he was in an Army hospital when he had come back from the European Theater. But he did not.

My father's death cost my uncle. I said so to my mother. She did not say no. She nodded with that poignant solemnness of hers as if an owlish wisdom was mine (or she was tipsy-like) though with her I could definitely go too far speculating. For my uncle, my father's absence would have been from the beginning a disaster but he was a really cheerful man and put what he had lost away among his values. His walk is different from my father's, toes out, shoulders high, looking forward to a good lunch with a buddy, an old buddy, the shoulders hunched a little. And high.

This was how my father was needed by the others. Bodily, I can say. "I don't know what to do with people who say something and go into gales of laughter," my mother said. "They're— it's my fault but—" I tried to think who else did it.

I had the power to keep the casket shut. I listen to my mother complain at having to yield to her mother-in-law and expose my father (if only here at the funeral home and not at the church); I found the simple fact already operative somewhere that I did have this power to keep the casket shut.

My mother is decisively angry at what she's not willing to fight.

In an elegantly tender, genteel person a deep, horrible anger crossed by the disaster of something like breaking a high heel off her shoe as she's walking along a dock to see a relative christen a mine sweeper during the war. But it comes out now (at me) in sorrow from the dramatic resources of her throat *and* in a sort of *sotto voce* that was akin to a moral hiss, as if her character was threatening her with a chemical shift that would absorb its former shadows.

Much of what was happening could seem trivial in memory. My mother must have moved from the front seat into the back seat when she and my uncle came for me from the hospital. Was she in the back while he drove from the hospital to the church? I see it's possible.

I wrote some few letters thanking people who wrote me during the first several days after my father's death. Also, I felt logy, stalled; and talkative, ready to be inspired by an amusing phone call from a friend.

People stood around near the shining contents of the casket—near *him*. Standing around with each other as if they knew what they could not say. An absolute stranger or two or three, who are these men? (Not the equal of my father, in the look of them, the feeling of vocabulary in their cheeks and noses and habits.) I am a person known without having to be introduced. My uncle speaks to me across a distance a little too great to have a conversation, and I nearly move toward him and the other man, as maybe I should. But my uncle undertakes to bring him to me, it's a matter of a few feet: "This is . . ."—and the man's first *and* last name . . . and then "Frank was an old and dear friend of your father's." I have a position, namable and understood, an apparently freeing fluid pomplike license that's mine. Yet so active, the force, and easy, so harshly O.K., and novel, that I do think I can tell what is going on: my father dead, my mother free if she would be, I alive as a voluptuous wind around me waiting to be appreciated, with a position, a magnetic halo, a mind, to be assumed forever from then on, but what were the vows? The affectionateness I gave to the people my uncle introduced me to could have been some harsh self I'd sensed gloriously near my shoulders, my shoes, but I let it take hold of me. I thought my father young for the first time. I believed his face, all but the eyelids baby-glued. I could have said so in that secretly festive company. I missed his back, his back view. I felt horribly sorry.

At this moment I do not yet know of the letter. And I didn't yet know from my lawyer-to-be schoolmate friendly-acquaintance that my father's body *belonged* to my mother, i.e., within limits of legal observance and obligation such as embalming and burial. What do I do? People stand around between the furnitured red walls and the figure in the middle of the room that is afloat upon a plush structure (I think of a ship-bunk bed, which it hardly is). And this structure and its contents appear *levitated* because I can't recall what the coffin is resting on.

Heavy furniture in red upholstery made heavier by low (but ugly and not *so* low) light though not so *light* as I remembered it, incandescent candle-substitute. Is *this* the funeral? What do *I* know? Actually I know everything, I haven't missed a thing. But I have. But I do know this is the "viewing," because I have been told by her when things were happening. And have heard the man tell my mother; and, actually, me.

A Visitors Book slanted on a lectern under a light remembered: "*already* remembered" was a sensation that settled abruptly into my belly without a doubt but like frivolity: both then and home again that evening with the phone ringing familiarly.

My father's fixed face, beautiful, out there in the "center" of the room, stood out exposed where his beloved mother wanted, who sat with her poor husband Pop on a couch parallel to the casket halfway back toward the draped window. A gentleman leaned near to her. "He was too young."

It is too clear, furniture in a room at the Home recalling furniture in another room because of the people in it. Let me let that furniture go its own way. My father's family at home seeming to be much less than they were because of routine that I grasped as comfortable and maddening routine, grasped lest they do something to me, detain me, slow me.

"I wish we didn't always have to go *there*." It's a speech, it has its prepared rhythm and end. But it sounds like a kid with specialized teenage if narrow confidence, does it not? But it's my mother speaking. But she was not alone. She was with me.

In that warm apartment, they gathered their armchairs into their entire action toward us: and my mother and I felt, to me at those times, one; also the high-legged, brittle settee; and crocheted antimacassars on the armchairs. *Old*, I thought these people: though Pop's wiry, a "boy"(!), springy, eleven years younger than Emmy, if somewhat aged (or tried) by her as he was also sometimes as amused by her ways; and I imagined these people waiting for our presence, not expressing it to each *other* eagerly but they were ready for our bodies and our sounds. Pop pulls open the front door: You're *late*.

My mother and I told the news, my mother was good to them, she didn't have to make up a thing. And active, light, thorough and affectionately amused all the way, charmingly factual and full for them. My grandmother asked after people she had never met, my parents' friends; remembering their lives, their habits, their families, their fall weekends at their summer homes, their parties; and asked by name, first name of, for instance, the man who had been to Oxford (pistols on the wall intricately simple, each with its own fascinating weight), friends of my parents who had come to pay their respects the day after my father died, standing as well as sitting in our living room, drinking. My mother did not evoke their voices, describe their clothes or powers. It was all for my grandmother mainly. Her missing him, my father, took a bodily pose: so that what I *could* see as subtly firm, religiously (I mean for the moment invulnerably) sentimental—and affectionately reproachful in a minor strain—is now what Emmy's *earned*.

They lacked my father. We, too, were without him but we'd been living with him. They needed us. It would seem my grandmother did. Then I wondered. Her grip on things was her pretty *manner*. A very social, to-the-hearing cheek-soft, but demandingly obvious manner of showing she was "sorry" or deeply sympathetically on your side or shocked, or twinklingly approving or absorptive. It was more slow-rhythmed than soft, it was a regret that she wasn't going to see you, more than trust that she would see you the next week and talk to you tomorrow or the next day, it was easy to call it a "hold" she had, for even my father, like my mother, called it (wryly) that: but it was force, that I felt in my mental return to it as a thing to think about, "cover" as if I were making strategic plans, plotting a many-dimensioned (or just dramatic) defense: she had a hold over her son, I did not think of my uncle then. I could have thought of it as "ability" but I felt it was a wave I would maybe get out of the way of, unclear to me only in look and measure because I didn't think enough about how I had heard it fondly and humorously mentioned, which might ruin humor itself for poor me at times.

I begin to *know* these things as I answer my mother's social anguish, the best care of her I take is find *her* truthfulness to tell her for *her*; until then, unsure who's influencing (as Pop said it) who, I saw that, after "the news" was done and the deft deed of kindness, and she's upset on the way home on the empty subway platform and, husky and tautly inward, sounding "through with them," yet so seriously tender and tenderly quiet to me, I'd forgotten in the midst of her feelings afterward—I'd mislaid the fact—a thing coming now up behind me very solid if I let myself just take it like that—that to her they brought him actually back; or, in her sense of responsibility, she *thought* they did. Terribly so, for *they* were *not* him, you could say, but "of" him. I actually know her face, the hollow of the throat, the attention of her eyes, their unwillingness to actually hold me, and know what *I* know but don't say and so don't have the experience of knowing—or haven't found how to *do* that particular thing yet. The main ones, my step-grandfather, and my grandmother, and my great-aunt and her daughter. "Of" him in body. They love my mother. She is "lovely" to them.

"I wish we didn't have to go *there*."

They did not bring him back for *me*.

They are going to the bathroom, the needlepoint toilet-seat cover, and on the white-tiled window ledge behind the toilet the saturated tiny yellow or purple sponge you pull out of the air-freshener bottle on a wire—I don't mean they are going to the john together but someone is going. Someone says, Have to pay a visit (have to pay a call). My mother's *language* recoils at theirs. Someone has a little gas. There's a joke about it. The table is set for tomorrow morning. Eight or nine small brown bottles of pills like a centerpiece on the crocheted mat.

"I wish we didn't always have to go *there*."

"We don't," is my answer. My contribution.

The letter's returned to me when the "handsome printing" came from my step-grandfather's shop in Manhattan.

I didn't look at the letter for weeks.

iii

When my grandmother and step-grandfather came to our house my mother wished they would be a little late. But I'm ready and wish in a way they would come. She hasn't been home from work long, she's nice to them, she does need to "unwind." They're outside our door right on the dot of five minutes early. That sounds like they didn't press the buzzer but produced some effect from the other side of the door, and thus waited until I opened up.

But they did buzz. Pop adds two short shots, which makes my mother say something humorous which was humoring herself. For the "other" reason she feels what she feels is nothing to do with work. It's "life," it's life's mysteriousness and hysteria, some plot and counterplot. *I* know: it's on aesthetic grounds she'd like them to be a little late. (She's just home from work and likes to sit with her drink and read the mail.) They like to eat early, which had to be *thought* about when they were having dinner with *us* (but *what* thoughts?) down in the Heights thirty minutes from where they live. An ounce of rash physical joy spreads into me suddenly and I fall to the floor-and-rug and do a few pushups. But he's on top of me. He's got his fingers on my neck, he's laughing, he's keeping me down as I push off against the floor, I'm crazy mad at him, I can't get him off my back. The bout is over. I can't take a joke. It wasn't one.

I did not always look forward to the visits in either direction. I throw at him an enemy invitation, a remark about taxes and politics knowing where he stands. But it comes out of my mouth humorous, yielding. After dessert, Pop yawns at shortening intervals until at last his yawn yields a reflective, soft cry, animal, ending in an unusually vague-eyed, perhaps self-accepting smile—family—knowledge. (Was it easier when my father was alive?)

The letter is away from me, my thoughts. And while I take up a copy of the "handsomely printed" letter with some wholeness or completeness of being overwhelmed and a fine stupidity like confidence or being on your mettle, the letter was at most dramatic. Not made up, with things fitted *in*to its decided custom like the Christmas sonnet, this letter is a very late New Year's missive, and dated Washington's Birthday years ago. My parents' friends speak of the letter. For them, too, it speaks. One man puts a shy hand on me to call it a "unique" letter, "very fine," as if to thank me for *writing* it. I have put the original away in my desk somewhere.

The "handsome printing" ensured the letter against loss. It was a corporate act. My father *said* to me that my mother and I and he were a corporation and I knew I would quote this sometime. In almost meaning that word "corporation," my father meant *us* to be his meaning—my mother and me: more than the word, the word conveyed love and what he had found himself settling for, and no matter how the word decays, and means to me "business" (which my father was not really in my opinion in), it conveyed much love. But is love "family"? The handsome printing preserved my father's letter in a stricter sense. I mean, *I* didn't "do" anything with that letter of his. Or not consciously. It had outnumbered me (if I cared); and I moved to one side of it, paper, words, and all.

Pop said, "Your father wrote extremely well," but it sounds like "Experience is the best teacher." I think, "He wrote with his feet! Like that guy that plays the piano! Who was in the newspaper!" I want to say, "He wrote with his *eye*balls!" I want to asininely say, "If it's *extremely well* we're talking about, *I am* extremely well."

I had a cold from the day of the funeral. Three days coming, three days here, three days going, according to my grandmother's sister, ever at home with her, my tall, subdued (but able to speak faster than my mother could feel) great-aunt Edna, thin, when she sat there on the sofa, and as her long-widowed wit and humility distract me, more truth distracts, "namely" that my *father* would have said "*exceedingly* well."

My mother by propagating that letter a month or so after his death fixed it as his letter. She did it jointly with his family, whatever she thought. His words were allowed to do it. Is the letter a belonging I am to reclaim? If words can't belong to us *from* someone else any more than our own can to us, my father's attention can. The letter was attention to me. Like a walk down along the docks. A talk. "To me, to me"—I did not think it easily, in the sense of precisely.

But long before this letter goes out, the other letters are coming in. To my mother; to her *and* me together; and some-times her and me on the *en*velope (which is a little new, or odd-*looking*). Three or four days after his death.

One says, "Please don't trouble to answer this letter. Consider it answered." This took me by surprise. It made me *want* to write an answer. I take at face value that man's effort. But I think (and thereupon almost tear up the shitting thing), "It's got a built-*in* answer, can you *do* that?, an automatic answer"; or "He's making rules for us, he knew what we were *feeling*—he sent the letter before we received it, he knew what we were feeling before we did, knew what had to be in our words before they came to us, before we wrote them." I hear them ready-made in me—he was way ahead of us, already there. I think, *You shouldn't have.* I thought: O.K., if I "consider it answered," *my* doing nothing about it is part and parcel of *his* having ... *what?* answered it himself? known what we felt? "Part and parcel," I thought again retreating. And does its being "answered" *already* mean that he is "with" us? I believe so, and for days I was moved by his saying "consider it answered," and it comes to me that I may remember it—if only writing a letter when someone dies; until now, when the words of that man threaten to take my meaning.

Who was he? Was that man more than saving us trouble? Saving us time and trouble, substituting for time spent writing him a few lines and licking a stamp and an envelope, the time set going by the fineness, unusualness (to me) of what he said. My mother, of course, answered the "letter."

The very *doing* was an answer, I thought, seeing her straight back sitting at the desk as I passed the wide, doorless doorway of the living room on my way out. I wrote down in a diary some trickery like, What if *I* answered him, telling *him* to consider *my* letter answered? For I was doing well, perfectly well—grades, girls, stories I was writing for the school paper, dive after dive I took off the worn, coldly raw cocoa matting of a too-stiff, one-meter springboard weekday afternoons to slip into the water as straight or secretly as I could—slide slow as a ship or great being into a wintry pool thronged with the belly-slap and chugging din of my teammates and, somewhere in my split-apart concentration, that overwhelming man-made ocean-factory noise of death.

I heard from the very first hours of my father's death that Time heals. Heard it from *my* minister on the Heights. He came that night swiftly. He's amazingly ready with the words. He means them. He's on the far side of the threshold, humbly (as if it's up to us to let him come in—whereas he once famously picked a gate lock at the airport when he was late for the plane and it was about to take off) and with (there, at first, at the door and in his black wool cape and its little chain across his collarbone never noticed by me before) a discretion that seemed, as knowledge, violent like some of the medicine of a doctor in an emergency.

He said a good prayer: I can feel it come clearly ("sent") through the outlandish apartment, where I must do something, make up something (to say the least): a man full of speech, portly, and imposing, he knew we were hurt and quietly quietly crazy, a man who parted *his* hair in the middle kindly like my dad. He said with eerie inadequacy that Time heals, yet he was working in a different time, I realized, my God! very *very* long time.

I heard it from actual other people as the next morning passed for us and whole highlighted days, tediously enchanted, fevered days followed again and again becoming days like today-and-yesterday at most, a group of days were like a day and a half; and the morning passes when my mother calls me into the living room where the desk drawer is out and she has an envelope.

Is it true, *Time heals all wounds?*, truer probably than all *I'm* not saying. Which wounds? Stabs? (The *skin* would be broken, I dawdled on.) A bullet skinning a temple? But I don't ask; don't care to know; yet do ask *myself*—do think this way— taking private steps; but not *thinking* much. Why do people use their mouths to say this sort of thing, their lips, dry outside (with soft and slick inside)? Dumb to ask—it's got an unsuccessful quality about it. There's a waste, a silliness, an importance only *made up* in my weighing *Time heals all wounds* (isn't that so?). Ungenerous not to just take those words, someone else's words "for it." Why stop everything and *say* them? Like some de-bunker. I'm of two possible trivial minds (one is more future, when I will look back)—but I mean: Either think, Yes it *was* trivial, petty—for my father said, Don't be a debunker—*Or,* Yes it was *O.K.* to ask, *Time?* and ask, *How* would it heal? and *What* wounds?

Her voice tipping downward, she says my name, and says it twice. She means, *Really!* which *is* more meant, and weightier than when at the dinner table in someone *else's* presence she says, "Oh *don't* say, 'O.K.' "—poignant and trivially enemy in its act—and her arch, though faint and painful, power gets me again—to lose my sense of humor except that it's still present, spread in this fixity of face of mine remembering how very gently she told him once that he had lost his sense of humor—when he was in the right if I recall.

I try to hear my father *react* to these speculations of mine, and get only my mother, dynamic and unsure, radiant, or dynamically busy, which was her poor form of sternness, at the desk, or cleaning the piano keys flouncing up and down (like a mad person playing by ear: which she nearly detests *my* doing— because she is a musician and doesn't play that way—or, I sometimes think, *can't,* though can play anything *from* the music and my father stands by her singing with me; *or* the sound of her cleaning the keyboard is one species of *talking,* finger-talking amplified)—till the phone rings and she leaves off as abruptly as she has been dusting swiftly (and *banging*) clusters of black and white keys. I know these things and might like a brother (*or* sister) to tell them to right now.

My mother let my father's memory enlarge by means of the letter. The thought of all those words of his did it. I was in my third year of high school, I was thinking about so much else.

I had the original of the letter back in my hands from my step-grandfather. When I got it home, I could have checked every punctuation mark against the handsomely printed version. But I didn't waste my time that way. Pop phoned one evening, asked to speak to my mother. I was doing my homework and she was playing the piano, partly for me. I could tell from her assurances to him that Pop was asking her what she thought about sending the letter to someone and that *she* felt he just wanted to talk to her.

People didn't ask about the original. Before too long I hardly knew where it was myself. If the letter is attention given to me, sending it out in all these copies is proof, or is giving *my* attention to those on the list.

I'm building backwards. *Do* I not know what's going on? How crushed Pop is at the viewing and almost kin to me. To his body before me in its suit I actually yield some of my un-employed spirit. I understand that he once shipped out to South America, and later, a young man from Maine, he married a beautiful Georgia widow in Brooklyn and took on her two young sons. I want to get away, yet this is the last time I can see my father's face. Someone said something in the warm room that got lost, but someone then said, "He's with *Him*." I am *not* horrified by the face—his head's hair on the pillow. And his ears. There's a decodable tincture of banana smell I've picked up before in this building. It stays with me as if someone has told me it is so. Someone said, "He was too young," and I hear, "He died too soon."

The funeral is tomorrow, so I've not received the letter yet. Pop does not know about the letter. I don't either.

My father all alight and amazingly close here still knows me. I believe this. I'd like to be alone with him—with my mother, too, but also alone myself with this body-face of my father, and it's so I can get to *be* alone—be *that*.

I hear, "He died too soon," I jerk my head around and feel that the person isn't there anymore who spoke, because I know that "*He was too young*" was what was said before.

"Too soon"—I didn't place the voice. (Days later the words come to me but scarcely any voice.) I'm horrified, or disgusted-scared, to think of this person before me who's not yet a doll-mannequin (who's a pink-cheeked young man who deserves his life) reading the paper, one leg crossed over the other, I hear the leg cracking. The face he wears I can believe is dreaming. It's a waste to try to say this isn't my father, because it is. "He died too soon," it was in the air, I don't place it, I have no plans. If this "body" isn't my father—as it isn't—but only isn't *quite*— then he may be someplace else. Is this getting funny?

I had heard of people being cremated. (Was it casket and all? With rabbit's foot and snapshots inside? a little blood left?) I kept a diary for a while, self-consciously, and then I stopped, a Christmas present from my parents. The pages felt a bit small, as if they fit into some case; I would get going and then that day would be finished. My father was buried. He has a closed-coffin funeral. Sometimes *ashes* are buried. My father believed in the resurrection of the body. He was buried in my *mother's* family plot in New Jersey under two maple trees (as his mother, Emmy, desires to be, who scarcely knows my mother's family). The wide straps of canvas cradling the casket over the grave like cargo moved a foot or so as if to show us what was going to happen after we left. My mother sat at the drop-leaf desk taking care of things for days. My father's company went on paying him. You could watch what happened, and you could think that my father hadn't "after all" died without the normal preparations. Coming down the hall I heard talk in the living room and realized the "him" was me.

I did not show the letter around. Nothing happened much at school. Some knew. It was no more noted than a birthday. My school acquaintance, the lawyer-to-be, asked how things were going. I thought I would talk of law. I said my mother's lawyers were old friends, so that helped. He shook his head. No, he said, you didn't want close friends as your lawyers. The advice didn't sting, and I didn't pass it on.

To some old friends I heard my mother say that my father's letter was "just like him." She spoke to others of my father's letter. She did not seem to get in the thing the way her in-laws did. They acted as if it belonged to "the family."

The Letter Left to Me

My father "was survived by" me, he left *me* to *them,* and maybe they couldn't count on that. You can't call the letter episode greed. I had some feeling I was being *honored* by my father's family. As if they knew not quite what to do with me. My father had been ten at *his* father's death. My mother did think of the letter as a thing my father and I shared—as ours. Like a deed, an outing, or a return on investment (though not like his salary). Like *reputation.* Was the letter mine by heredity? She has pondered its *words,* bless her; a copy was on her bed table, folded in the middle sitting up against her water glass. Let the margin halo light the page in the deepness of her dark drifting, she read the sentence-by-sentence words that were there and heard the voice of him.

I saw the letter starting out a long distance away and being here just on time. "*I* couldn't have said it better," the husband of that old-friends couple she was speaking to about the letter said. So "it" was an existing thing: to be aimed at, not said *until* it was said. His wife said to me, "You couldn't have had a better father." There was a section of very slightly brown-colored skin down the side of her neck, not actually bad to look at. She made me in a gingerly way think. "The truth is" (as my father himself once said) *I* didn't *have* another father.

My uncle was now getting settled. His wife and small son were with her family hundreds of miles away. For a while soon after my father died, my uncle lived with us. It was closer to Wall Street than "Mother and Dad's." We had a guest room with a separate bathroom. It was at the far end, the foyer end, of our big apartment. He had been attached to the Eighth Air Force and had briefed bomber pilots before their missions and had been on a few himself. He had almost had to have his arm amputated in a hospital in Dayton, Ohio. My father said they had used a dirty needle on him. My uncle had attained the rank of major before being discharged. He was working in Wall Street. One evening we're waiting in the living room for my mother to finish cooking dinner, and I'm irritated with my uncle. He's reading the paper and I have nothing to say. Even I was more mortal-seeming to myself than he; he was there, across from me: he was thinking something negligible, his own death hadn't occurred to him. He called Pop "Dad."

I took up a small book lying on the table; it was on stock-market economics, it was new-looking, the cover olive-green with fine black lettering. I might as well have been reading it upside down. I did, though, read two pages to "show" my uncle, and he looked up and noticed the title, I think.

One day I came home and Gertie was there and told me my mother was with the doctor, she wasn't feeling well. Gertie spoke confidingly, she spoke fast and quietly, but in or inside herself she was (*I* knew) at a slow pace—which was an honor of kindness and was her nature. A tall, lean-cheeked man with cool, helping hands was this doctor of ours, an elder of my church on the Heights, and he came out now as if to talk to me. He had given my mother a sedative. He explained this to me not Gertie. My mother was upset, he said, but she was all right. She had been "hysterical." I went to her, not able to imagine this.

She was lying down and she was breathing too deeply. I had almost never seen her cry, it would be like destruction of her face, I half-imagined, but I was very wrong. I didn't know what to do. She said, "Your father was so fine, he was so fine."

She wanted my uncle gone. I *more* than felt for her. I wasn't *doing* anything. I looked out the window, I'd been swimming at school, diving over and over again. I touched her, I said he didn't have to stay. I was speaking truth but it wasn't mine, I mean understood and not stale words. I felt desperate—that it was too soon, but my words could be final. I want to do something. I had seen her cry when I had said something irritated to her when we were waiting for the elevator downstairs coming home from the grocery store just a few days ago, and I had seen her cry four years ago when my aunt phoned to tell her their mother, my New Jersey grandmother, was dead. I knew that my mother was admirable. Did *she* have to do something "with" *me*?

I did things with my mother. I sit around with her friends, go to a restaurant; once in a great while think, This is what's actually happening. Two organists came to the apartment and were hilarious—talented professional musicians, they all carry on and someone calls my mother "brilliant"; or she has season tickets for the Boston Symphony in Brooklyn and I am dangerously drowsy during the most beautiful music; and let me make no mistake—this questioning accumulates—for it's that—my mother took a job before the end of the year and still was home fairly soon after *I* got home from school, glad to have the place to myself, to write sometimes lines and lines in my diary called forth *by* my diary, with its too small pages. A subway ride from far out in Brooklyn for me, a short one under the river for her (they're equal) or she walked the Bridge, stylishly, with men she had known for years. And she praised me in her way *and* must have troubled herself over not laying down the law. What was there to lay it down about? My beginning to come home late? She was truly busy with great grace and with a mainly secret hecticness.

I let myself be interviewed for a scholarship to Harvard. I thought I wanted a small college. I don't put Harvard down as my first choice. It passes—this time of choosing or not choosing. My classmate who was going to be a lawyer has decided on Princeton. I could not see him there, though we were not close friends. We were on the school paper, where between ourselves we swapped superior witticisms at the expense of the faculty adviser. I understand physics but can't do the problems. We competed in English, where we were waiting for class to start when he said he had heard of a letter my father had written to me. *Heard?* I asked. He named one of our teachers who had received a copy of it. I didn't know of this. What I said was that some copies had been made of the letter. (I thought I saw lightly pushing at my classmate's mouth a word, as if it sounds in his clear, "very good" mind. Like swashing a glass of something in somebody's face, a fantasy barraged me that I was in my grandparents' living room saying to all of them except my mother, who was nonetheless there, what I never had said. The word I thought my classmate was thinking was *Why?—why* had copies been made?) He *said,* It must have been a good letter.

I said, "Why?"

"Well, that's a question, too," he says, oddly.

But yet another daydream (this one international, familiar, so moving)—this revealing my father's real whereabouts—comes to trouble and entertain me again and be dropped summarily from sight, and I have no father to not tell it to for I know what he would say.

I said the teacher hadn't mentioned the letter to me. (This fact now fascinated me somewhat.)

Mr. Romine had written to me, hadn't he? my classmate said.

About my father's death, I said; and spoke to me about it—asked me how old my father was (I added, remembering, and I'm underlining in my notebook words written on the board yesterday by the teacher, so that I remember my father saying one night in my room, looking over my shoulder, that you shouldn't underline all the time).

Class has started and my classmate alters his voice to report what Mr. Romine said: that to write something like that so far in advance it must have meant a lot to him.

He wrote it too soon, I said, as if I had thought this through, and the white-haired teacher pointed a finger of chalk at me and cocked one black eyebrow. (I could be called on when my mind was, supposedly, someplace else, I always heard the ques-

tion.) I proposed to myself discussing later with this smart classmate the familiar words that visited me now, *It was too soon*—
as they had on the evening of the viewing after someone said,
He was too young.

The words *too soon*—my father had lost all these years of
time, these weeks, weekends, a year of newspapers including the
News of the Week current events quiz on Sunday. But I mean
his friends, his family, his thoughts, his churchgoing.

I could not have discussed the words with Pop. Emmy,
though, would say in a tone of serious face-to-face intimacy at a
visit or over that telephone she knew so well, that I have been
under a strain and maybe somebody at the funeral home *did* say
that, for she would now think *she* had heard it said; and it was
true, you know, "your father" *was* too young, too young to go.
A cardboard stationery box in the living room at my grandparents' held many copies of the letter. My mother kept ours in the
desk. I was definitely young. But was I not *too* young? *He* was
too young. Maybe *I* was too *soon*. I wept uneasily. Not fully, not
with that pleasure. It was in my room. It was not real grief-
pain grief-hopeless. But an inquiring force of crying for the letter.
I took up three of Pop's printed copies and spread them out in
both my hands so that to my eye they looked each different
from the others. They could not be answered. I was on the loose
in my own willingly uncomprehending fashion.

Yet my father's death put me to sleep: to myself I have voiced,
virtually audibly, truths that I have troubled to figure out—then
not *acted* on them. (Who hasn't done this? I guess I don't know.)
I said to myself that I had gone to sleep; it came out in thought,
but I doubted that idea. Soon after my father's death I said it
to the dark-haired, radiant-cheeked girl, the one I loved the
night my uncle came to the church to get me. Actually I was in
love with her, and I wanted to do nothing but kiss her there at
the church at the very moment I was told my uncle was downstairs, though I also thought of the slow length of my tongue

taking minutes to pass over her nipples one by one which I had never seen or touched.

My father lying in the hospital was in my mind like a perhaps fine snake under a stone that evening, but like a new ability I could let wait, and I had gone to the party at my mother's urging and was in bliss. But the *quality* of her urging—I felt it—a timelessness in it. I had had a hard week of missing school to be at the hospital, where I had "been," or "hung around," mostly in the hall, out of my depth but necessary, perhaps to my mother. Or to myself. Or to my father.

I later told that girl the sleep idea, and she believed it, I think to some further point of understanding than my own. If I had admitted to her that I didn't believe *myself* in this matter, she might have helped still more. Her mouth possessed a curve, a flowery flare that she didn't do anything to create, and her mouth was not wet, it seemed fruitful. I found when I kissed her for the first time some days later that her lips weren't closed tight when she kissed. I moved my upper lip a little downward to this soft opening with an inward breath and a small unsticking. Then it didn't seem so open, and I moved my *lower* lip *up* into the soft parting and felt crude and summerlike. We were in a brownstone doorway in our overcoats and the stoop lights come on. I felt that something was obvious, too much so. *She* was, or *it* was. But her settled tenderness had in it fun, not compassion exactly. Another fellow liked her, and he was a friend of mine, and there wasn't enough pride in my valuing. And from that time little magic. That was it, yet I loved her, or liked her, and I did not see all that there was to *that*.

Yet without a thought, a month later, actually when the letter was being printed up, I picked up the phone to call her to ask her to come to the Sportsmen's Show. But my mother stopped me; it was Pop's invitation to *me,* she said.

I went to the Sportsmen's Show in Manhattan with my step-grandfather, it was our fourth or fifth annual time, we had a *good* time and we did not speak a lot. Pop told me to rise up springily on my toes when I walked, don't clump down on ya heels. The logrolling in a tank was the feature that we had to check on the time of and talked about looking forward to for the humorous violence of the men bopping each other and getting drenched in the tank. Two men equipped with poles with rubber ends tried to knock each other off a log. There was a four-man event as well, the logs spinning as if slowly, then like machines, as the men trying to stay on top of them ran faster and faster to stay on. It was a Maine counterpart of bronc riding, it recalled some real, or useful, activity, but it wasn't as bad as it looked, it had this treadmill dimension, but I liked the sheer *action,* the men in the tank there below us at a distance electric and distant in their initial tentative balancing and their clothes and their bodily nerve, like hockey players at Madison Square Garden who were more real at the gigantic wide distance of a paid ticket; and it was the motion of the heavy log in the resiliently different water.

But in that echoing indoor space I gravitated more than Pop knew to the tableaux of the equipment companies. All that new gear. Better than a tennis shop. Tents taut and staked out, fishing rods in full racks, axes, accumulated wonders, fake grass and pine—a man and woman in green-and-black lumberjack shirts, a woman in high waders, they were prophetically lifelike, in fact moving figures, talking quietly as if behind glass. Pop asked if they still made one fly rod, he'd exchange a genuine pleasantry grinning about where they were from and where he had spent time. He introduced me. (We were very near Pop's printing shop.)

The Sportsmen's Show! It gave us things to talk about, though we didn't really. What was it that we looked at together? It was outside us. He was on home ground. It was Maine come to Manhattan. No jump at all. There was a printed program. I read it to Pop. The print gave the events a wild future. It was this vast lower exhibition space right near Grand Central Station, in a vast basement floor of a mere hotel, all right; but it could be the north country, and for both of us. I was asked what I wanted to see, and Pop said *he* wanted to visit the canoe display, he was hoping to order one for the place in Maine. It was not like when I saw him at home. I don't want to even think about the other "home ground."

There he was on the spot—needed, catered to, tired, opinionated, habited with a security sounding all round with female tones. Though it was he who "held forth," which of course was not the only talking, or even the most time-consuming.

There is a lot of talk, and there are pauses, those evenings. I'm older, less alive to their welcome, the humble things of their life, I talk about my education, I put words together as if they're my thinking. The windows take your eyes, the reflections, the coffee table, the rug, the little lamp table, a radio that's never turned on while we're there and underneath it a V-rack that held several books. He does not know his own nerves, his fingertip that he scratches with a fingernail with a look and care of consciousness, scratches finely at for years at a time to peel away dry skin—callus *maybe,* but I did not think it was callus. My mother minded his doing it, she fusses, standing on the subway platform, while I am in the future and foresee coming home from college for an occasional weekend, Christmas-like after travels. What does she imagine I'm thinking about?

I drove up to see a certain college with my mother's friend and *his* son, who in the end decided against going. It was a "small college." I'm the bright guest. From that visit I recall the town but do not imagine what I may *do* in it (or *with* it).

Isn't it like a boarding school? I visited one once for an entire weekend to stay with the son of still other friends of my parents (who had *introduced* my parents). That single boarding-school weekend I kept a survival lookout on my own behalf moving through the military morning air, harshly your own.

You walked up a path to a brick building where you might have only one class and then go outside and next door to another building.

My step-grandfather reported of a cousin's son—cousin by marriage—that he planned while still in grade school to go into the insulation business, building supplies, and so forth. When I scorned planning he said, "Well," it was better than *not* planning.

But I'm not innocent. "He has such a fine mind," my grandmother confides to me in the kitchen. I'm going to carry in a plate of (*they* call them) "appetizers," cut circles constructed of concentric rings of white and whole-wheat bread stuck together and spread over the top with a pink or lime-colored spread. She means he has educated himself, has "lived" without much formal education. She means he will fix the faucet, do accounts; has the facts. She means he can be relied on for answers. Answers often in *action*. He is drawing up plans to build a cabin on his lake land that will help pay for the main house. I do listen. I wish my father were here to talk. In the living room my great-aunt Edna, who has been reading the paper, asks gauntly, cheerfully, "What's the news?" I could tell her some murder I read about in a *Daily Mirror* left on my subway car. But I have this terrific inkling "once more" that my *life* might elapse without my acting on it: that I have a free power (free beyond fighting) and it's to do with seeing what has happened and will happen—planning the thing, no less. But instead I report to Aunt Edna (my *great*-aunt—Pop calls her "Edna") that I have an editorial in the school paper. Can it *be* soon after my father's death? It can.

"Clear writing is hard work," Pop says. "You've got to know what you're talking about. You've got to have something to say." What is the "experience" he's always talking up? Is it writing copybook maxims in school? I missed my chance to answer his "know what you're talking about," but I don't have more than a clue what I'd say. (He shields his match to light, to actually burn the *end* off, his Lucky Strike, while I check his brushy old moustache; he kills the fire with a two-finger-and-thumb snap, really only the middle finger making the snap against the heel of the palm.)

I'm not smoking in their presence yet, of course. I "wouldn't think of it." Pop really enjoys the cigarette itself, and the smoke filtering through his nose hairs, his head (his ears). Pop does not speak of what he failed to do in the past. I get him onto Fulton Lewis, Jr., the conservative radio commentator, because it galls me. Aunt Edna tells me after a while that she likes the man's voice but not him. Pop intones his long "Well" that sounds like "Whale."

I'm in our guest-room bathtub at the far end of our apartment, soap dissolving in the water in front of me. I found I had studied their voice mannerisms, word meanings, but, more, *instances*—an experience I acquired as irritation, also fiendishly close attention. ("You fiend," I say to myself.) But days later I don't link these passions with learning.

Brooklyn where *they* live isn't Maine *or* Manhattan. Their album of snapshots if I get it out they gladly joke about. They murmur as if their voices were partly far away in the photo. There's Pop shyly stern in rough flannel breeches—olive-green I know they are. And me, at seven, holding up a dead lake trout suspended near my head, a beached rowboat behind me, ready to go: Pop gave me credit for landing that fairly infrequent fish though not fighting fish (not yanking, lunging, squirming, digging, dodging), and it was the same day I hooked a dark, strong eel, strange as a tire on the end of the line, till the greatness of its weight communicated itself suddenly as having been a subtly lashing force down there. Emmy's in another snapshot, a pale, white-haired, tentatively standing, small, softish, alert-eyed, frowning, smiling "person" in a print dress and white cardigan sweater, capable then when I was a small boy of making *me* wear, mortified, her near knee-length pink woolies when the weather-wind thickened into storm one late, gray afternoon after fishing.

From my mother I derived a bodily idea that these people were not *my* family, or main and natural family, while knowing in a potentially discomfited, encompassing nearness of smell or alien pace, that they *were Family.* It was how they saw themselves, though not Family to just anyone (though always interested in visitors, my grandmother at least); I saw that you might let people *tell* you how to see them. Though do you then agree?

My feelings about them were not snobbery. Not because I cared about them. But because my irritations with them were sound. I wanted to be surprised when I went to see them, or to be let be, as I was at my other, New Jersey grandmother's, where there were three floors, an attic, and a large yard. My mother and I enjoyed agreeing about them on the walk to the subway. We *were* snobbish, but we also weren't. When I left after a visit I could feel it was like an amount or quantity of money in the bank.

I want to write Pop. About how the letter was railroaded through. To tell him, to hopefully enlist him as the listener, to be his grandson. He'd answer. But he will say that he for one does not see why I wouldn't want others to receive my father's food for thought. Do I already agree with that?

"*I* think we're good friends," my mother has just said, cutely in public, quizzically, a bit slowly. Others are present at our dinner table, it's late and I have geometry to do, and it is me she speaks of, several weeks after my father's death, more than "us"—more, I see, than *herself,* the gently arch source of this idea regarding mother and son friendship. So with her hospitality I feel her fear. Somebody says, "That's as it should be," and I suppose (thinking heavily, quickly, stupidly) it *is* "as it should be"—but I think I don't show it. And I now don't change the subject *or* carry it on, which I have found I have plenty of power to do, because there is no other male living in this house. But I see I had this *before* my father's death, but I take it back—I didn't. I'm known for having been outspoken "as a little boy"—known in "the *family*." But now at this dinner table full of enemies, I only *think*, "You shouldn't have, you really *shouldn't* have pretended that *I* thought we're not friends."

My vision of this woman at the other end of the table is moving all over the place. I would not say the words "How *could* you" because I couldn't follow them up with anything and I'd be afraid how *I'd* feel after hurting *her* feelings. Let me, though, put it as an accounting. I might do that. She has been good to me. She *is* good. I will not figure it out yet. Our little predicament brims—it runs quite strongly along and is high tension beside all this squashed, after-the-crisis silence in the muscles.

A closeness founded on *no* speech? This is uneasy but is an idea—a *some*time closeness. But when we are doing the dishes at eleven-fifteen on this school night, and she's not so rippling and floating, not at all silly (is it because of *me*?)—and just before she I know is going to say, of the hot-soaped plates *I'd* considered *rinsed* but *she* has poured steaming *water* over in the drying rack, Just leave those—why, she tells me (with relief, I think), that she had a "nice note"—she meant to show it to me—from Mr. Romine about "the letter." I reflect on what's been said, the interest if any this evening, and I turn my sight of this woman into words such as what the hell is *she*? It is an awful set of words and readily answered, "Someone" I love—and admire, too. For all she can gracefully do, and for the admiration she receives.

The letter left for me. The letter left. In a drawer of a drop-leaf cherry-wood desk I unknowingly had sat at. Though the letter had spent time in the safe-deposit box across the river as well.

She returns my look, we are earning generally the same life right now. "I'm glad you sent it to him," I say and mean it,

though can't get out "Mom" at the end. The phone's ringing—
Did I say what I said?—and she leaves the kitchen by the
swinging door into the dining room. It couldn't be "the Family"
calling; they're in their beds by now.

What am I waiting for?

My classmate who was going to be a lawyer played "testing"
games with his father. Catch questions, logic, math. (But I *knew*
what happened to my fist when I opened my hand.) He was
very spunky, had money in his pocket, which he didn't care
much about—wasn't tight about it—had dollar bills in his
pocket—next to his leg—not with a money clip like my step-
grandfather. My father had spotted me a queen at chess. My
classmate laughed derisively at this but it *made* him laugh. One
day out of the blue he asked where my father had attended
college.

I think he *meant*, How are you feeling these days?

It made me see my father skinny in his grave.

He said his father had bought him a hundred shares of
General Electric stock. I thought this meant he knew my father
was in Wall Street. We had analyzed atrocity photos, seemingly
years ago.

In general, I did not think about the final months before I
went to college as a time when things "needed my attention." I
decided against signing up for ROTC. I did not want to give
up one college course to so-called officer training and commit
two years to the Army upon graduation. Pop said I should write
them and find out more before I decided.

My mother's musician friend to whom I had said that my
father had "passed away" came for dinner and thanked me for
sharing my father's letter. Her old bushy-haired husband was
my mother's mentor, he's said to be slated for a symphony-
orchestra-conducting job in Florida, I have seen him conduct in
a barn in Massachusetts in a short-sleeved white shirt rehearsing
and talking and singing all at once. His wife is here alone. She

says it was an "excellent" letter as if *I* had written it, and I thanked her, and out of my mouth came a thought: "I don't know what I would have thought if I'd found it before he died." My mother said my name, I did not answer to it. I wanted to argue, but to silence her. My mother's friend said that that was very interesting. I had the impression that I closed the subject. My father will say, "The subject is closed." He will say, "Less noise from the cheap seats."

My classmate the lawyer-to-be was tired first thing in the morning, he went to bed when he felt like it, always had. I wondered if this was Jewish. I said my father had waited up for me when I came back late from a party; he was angry, my curfew had been midnight.

"When was *that*?" my classmate asked.

"Two Christmases ago," I said, and he said, thoughtfully, "Just before he died." I mentioned with light, actual nostalgia the girl I had been at the party with. I was thinking of plans into which others fit.

He asked if my *mother* got after me. She was awake usually when I got in, I said; his questions or maybe my answers were pretty close to home, I wasn't going to tell how she called my name asking if it was me, and then after I was in bed with the lights out I would hear her footfall and know she was past my father's bed, and hear the bathroom door shutting very firmly against the sticking of old layers of paint and then the toilet flushing and surging for an instant as the door opened. He said, "You're the only guy I know who thinks about *little* things—I mean, you need at least one friend who thinks about little things," he said, his slant mysterious to me, or lame.

"Well, we're not really *friends*," I said.

"Oh I think we *are*," he said—"*I* think we are." He wasn't a person who repeated himself. He said things and that was it. "My father and I have arguments to tear the house down," he said.

"We're not having an argument," I said.

"What about when you came home late?" he said.

I had been waiting for months to say, *You've* seen the *letter.* But I had not asked point-blank.

You think you can do better, I thought.

He shook his head, as if to say, *his* fault for not conveying what he meant. "Sorry," he said, polite.

"You *are* a friend," I said, letting this say whatever it did. For it was he who had advised me on Custody of the Body and on keeping "a certain distance" from your lawyer. My eardrums attacked like battering rams. Which they did when I got myself into something I had to see through, like affronting one of my elders. Would our teacher have shown him the letter? I asked if Mr. Romine had told him what was in my father's letter. Only that it mentioned Lincoln, and it was a *good* letter, my classmate replied.

In relief, I admired him, my blood was up. "I think you've seen it," I said, to see what would happen.

"Not me," he said. "But, I mean, it was printed up, wasn't it? Well, he must have said some things in that letter."

"My father said he hoped I would turn out to be a better man than he was," I said.

"I've heard that one before," my classmate said.

"Who from?" I said.

"You fool," came the answer with a power I wished to take as also mine, "*you* know what you're doing."

iv

We were at school five days a week waiting for graduation. I learned from a friend that as long ago as last year a classmate had let it be known that he wouldn't consider a bid from the fraternity this friend of mine was about to join if *I* was given a bid. This last year, then, had withheld a fact underlying perhaps all that had been going on. Yet no more than that, and it was almost over. The admired classmate joined another fraternity; so did I.

Without devoting himself to a subject, without a worry in the world, he was smart. It was like a talent for tennis, *his* talent for tennis—timing taken for granted with abandon, easy-looking repetition that people don't find boring. We've got a quiz in Solid, it's rough, it's solid geometry, the unforeseeable future, the hour's up: I hide my relief, *or* that I am *not* relieved, as he and I, briefly together, move down the old hall, supposedly transformed, parrying small challenges with small challenges that have to be taken lightly like jokes, about problems and answers that have a dimension of dreadful depth for me: he so knows what *is* important and what no *longer* is—is that it? it's some secret, I've decided (and decided with an asinine embroilment of my own force and interest, which seem young or negligible next to him).

He would succeed when he needed to. That astonishment at just things having happened—that wasn't his way—the slowness of an army's movement in Europe; how "the" Indians habitually *wasted* the flesh of the bison, as our American History teacher fiercely emphasized on a page of our book much underlined by all of us; the displacement of volume you could take a simple measure of.

Facts which might be just my comfort in the page—an appetite making mysteries of the schoolroom menu or exotic endlessness. Were others like me? This admired classmate whom I could not, except secretly, think of as a friend, was *business*like.

He had "money in his pocket," yes, I hear myself saying it like one of my elders last weekend in my mother's living room; and he was humorous, subtly cheerful; did not *need* to get mad— he was "in power." He had friends, as I had, but he was literally surrounded by friends, often passing down those old halls with their yellowed-glass transoms and greasy-grained wood floors from class to class with a regular bodyguard—including, until his older brother graduated, his brother's friends too. Did he catch on sooner—I mean, to what was going on, or worth knowing? Word filtered down to us about IQ records in the registrar's office. His was supposedly right up there with the three or four Jewish boys at the top. Some parents—his father was a doctor—had exercised their rumored right to know, whereas I had not known which if any of the intelligence tests we were given from time to time without warning had *been* the IQ. This classmate was going to his brother's college—the college I was now apparently bent on making mine. This was in part *why* I was going.

It's a relief to leave for college. The fear in it is a relief. Long before I set out, I see the faces of people there. They make sounds, laughing and revealing. I foresaw dropping in on my teachers in their offices in buildings that looked like private houses. They welcome me. I arrive with written things.

This was not too far from what really happened, and we were addressed, as in high school, by our last names. I show up in a bewilderingly *young* professor's office. I sit, I make up perilous things to say: "But the purpose of a political party isn't *only* to get elected." We called the course "Poly Sci." My high school we had called "Poly." He spoke in class of ideas waiting to be used. This excited me, but I do not say so in his office, it has something for me, I am free to be perhaps destroyed. I asked questions that I realized I could have answered *myself* at the instant they came off my vocal cords. I visited his office and could think of nothing to say until, as a thought (or words) came to me at last, *he* said that the hardest thing to learn was how to follow an idea out fully. This felt awful, though he had said it in our class—which I saw was a reason to *go* to class.

I passed through days of thinking again how to *talk*; to devise or *come upon,* and give back, worded statements out loud worth answering. Or to say anything at all. I was eager, and not convincingly friendly necessarily.

I looked up from the Quad, freshmen were seated casually fitted into the third-floor windows talking back into the dark acoustic exclusiveness of their rooms, calling down into the Quad, passing the time of day. To a fellow down the hall I introduced myself, first name, last name; and he answered "Hell*o*" plus *both* these names of mine like a riposte or joke I had overlooked, or a fault now that I was in the big time. Yet he was humbly informative, man to man, and it turned out he was already planning to go to Germany next year by student ship.

I knew the mileage between here and New York City, but I did not make it equal some other things *about* it, time, noises, money, always noises, sleep, a countryside between here and the city atomized by some disorderly dream of mine, a bird upside down on a tree trunk, black-and-white, its head black-and-white-striped, its *cheeks* black: "What's it good for?" I would hear Pop state, and he might know the name of that living bird:

the right-angle curve twenty miles south with the yellow-and-black barrier, a freshman, elegant, piloting his parents' car, who died Sunday night of our fourth weekend—a life of four weeks—and I in detail envisioned my mother receiving news of my death, and swiftly made up a letter received after my death and saw her reading it.

I did not study well—with the right speed. Yet I did not go my own way either. But study *what*? There's a general minor petty dissoluteness around here within a narrow range, and I'll avail myself of it. Artistic girls not subject to curfews exist at a college not far away across the state line if one had a car. That is, there was a girl there who was the friend of a friend. Against this, in language and professors' quirks, stood an enforceable new force of custom, intellect, academic Fate—worth actual *money* (I see for myself, yet little further than this) and as fine and unavoidable as the landscape. But I have already felt it at Poly in the voice—and the eyes and, on his head, the oversized hornrims—of my colorful classmate the lawyer-to-be correcting me on "the Battery," that area at the southeast tip of Manhattan: for God's sake didn't I know it referred to *gun* battery?—the English had placed cannons there, where the ferryboats left for Staten Island—"taking thought for the future," he had oldly said, rolling his eyes, puzzlingly.

Somewhere in my system I had kept going a plan of action, be it ungrasped by me. Vague as my father would immortally tolerate in his son.

I'm early to class and never seem to stop thinking, or start.

I make up again the story in my head called Custody of the Body. Left to my step-grandfather to see what *he* would make of it, he surprises me by giving my dad's body to Harvard but then it's no surprise. After that it was left to the ROTC here at college. It was accorded a drumbeat ceremony, I was there.

Then it was left to the girl I had loved and now still loved. *She* sat with my father for days, and would kiss his forehead next to the scalp line in the middle where his hair was parted. She watched him with concern, her tears watering his eyelids, his eyelashes dark, until one spring evening at sunset he *opens* his eyes.

Then it was left to me. The doctor at the bedside said to the woman and her son, "I'm sorry." The face on the pillow already seemed altered. A bomber passed low near the hospital window, guttural and encompassing. My father had been unfit for even limited service. The woman turned to her son. She would not want the coffin open. The son, backing toward the doorway and turning to go, felt it did not look like his father but could not say no to his mother, and she could hardly speak to him.

My early thoughts on what had really become of my father reinstated themselves. They're suitably distant and international, and irresistibly not true. I've never put them down on paper before. He's walking on the other side of the street. I'm at the corner by the Plymouth Pharmacy—the names won't change— on the Heights, across from the high hotel that boasts a ship's restaurant at the top, and I'm across the intersection from "the paper store." All may be changing except the old names. Do we reach the place because of a tingling obligation in the event?

My father was spirited away on a government mission. No one else would do. He was seeking information, but seeking some overwhelming agreement: it's in a typed statement, a folded piece of paper: he's seeking to *do* this by the most delicate negotiation, postwar, global. Not even his family must know. Least of all his family. He had gone somewhere in central Europe. A foreign assignment so delicate his family would not be told: the risk was great to him, greater than to his wife in her grief.

He would be out of sight for months. The community of nations ranked somewhere outside family. This was a grand and awful way to be a citizen, to be a member of the community of nations. I engineered the daydream, I toured the Displaced Person (DP) camps. Wherever I was, he was away. The war seemed not over after all. Exhausted and dirty, he was disguised by unimaginable mishaps, I had to protect his poor body, but he really was a quick mover. Yet I saw him showing up one day. It makes it*self* up. He came back so naturally, he simply *was* back. As if he *had* been *away* but knew he was coming back.

Now, at this late date, it might be here, to this new town. I had known he would return, hadn't I? Surely it was no surprise. She should marry again, I've heard. I try to ask my father in a dream. An organist friend of my mother's says, If she enjoyed it first time around, she'll try it again. But what if that's *true?* Either way I don't want to be around.

Some droll types trooped in and out of the dormitory rooms I shared. Many seemed at home, those first summery days, while it was the air, the trees, the visible mountain that were mine like real estate. Vague, and "behind" me, a plan, a line of action has been maintained through the months of my father's death. My mother would write me and she would phone every three or four days.

Pauses came into her calls, as if something's happening at that end that may be up to me. She phones uncertainly and yet over-emphatically as if I'm expected to not *only* talk. Then I am quietly-silently taken to task, I think, yet in a way congratulated—on some luck or other. So I came to feel a potent hypocrisy upon me—that's what it was. One night she was slow and pausing, and complaining, tired from her job and an after-work retirement party. And she had to go out to the "family's" tomorrow night—which, from where I stood outside the city, was quite a while ahead; and "Pop's already talking about next summer"—she made a new *sound,* high or whining, passing or theatrically light or slight. Which I then remembered, for I had once taken action when she had said she wished we didn't always have to go *there,* and my answer was "We don't."

But over the phone, conversation may end.

I get off the phone unfinished, extended within myself tight, relieved, and go straight to my room to type a letter to her. *Was* the high sound new? Could it be *not* new? Was it old? It scares me. Her letters have news in them. They're active reports, they are her, they are cheerful, but I know them to be melancholy in their civilized factualness. Phoning and writing, some idea came with all that easy-come-easy-go I had learned from my elders' jibes to locate merely in my brain.

I write her that night, that instant. Do I betray my cruelest vision? I write once a week, maybe every five or so days. I heard loud laughs from the hall as I typed the letter and knew it was the fellow who was often on that pay phone. He had both his parents on the line sometimes, they had two telephones at home, he was the one who had said both my names back to me like a lesson when I had introduced myself.

Presently, in midsentence I went out and he was gone. Two players huddled at cards were visible through a door partly ajar, and I knocked on his door, which he sometimes, irritatingly but impressively, left wide open when he had someone in for a drink before dinner. He was deep in his sagging old armchair, one leg over the other, reading a small green-cloth book, compactly solid, a Shakespeare play. He looked at me. I verified tomorrow's calculus. I inquired if he had learned anything more about student ships going to Europe next year. He shook his head as if I were making conversation. No, but those German cities would be something to see, what was left of them. I asked how often he wrote home. (Had I gone too far? I didn't *know.*) He shrugged like a joker: "My parents would think something was wrong if I started writing," he said with that flair like an intelligence he didn't show off, which to me felt conjured and wantonly true or like lies but wasn't.

Some people phoned instead of writing. I was finishing a book by Dostoevsky without quite attending to the political side.

The book had not been assigned. Given my courses, it *could* not have been. I had discovered it. I had never heard of it. It was disapproved of by a teacher of mine, to whom I mentioned it. He said it was just peddling ideas. He said the title wasn't the most accurate translation. He asked me what I had gotten out of the book. I said—but I was startled—that in it people's servants carried letters back and forth any number of times a day in that town. My teacher said, Good, he had never heard anyone say that about the book.

He was talking so that I who knew less would understand, I said it had a universality that went beyond the time it was written in, and my teacher smiled and inquired what time we were living in *now,* and I said, Early postwar, but he said, Why not early *pre*war? His words sent me away proud.

These "day" letters servants delivered breathed violence— was it "vile*ness*"? Day after day, twice a day it seemed, these written reactions threatened to be final, they couldn't be just answered then and there, could they? Or maybe, *in* this flow of heartfelt malice, they *could*! Returning down the hall I knew how some people would rather write than phone, and, without grasping or striving to grasp it, I would have liked to ask my teacher that, but it wasn't the thing to ask him. The later parts of that Dostoevsky book I saw were more made up, more planned.

I ended my letter to my mother. I had inveighed against those who would expect me to be one thing or another. I knew this had been boring. My nerves increased the vagueness I let ravel them, amassed things I could not reach even the *feeling* of not being able to say. My reading comes inevitably into my letter—this unassigned Russian novel *The Possessed. The Demons* it could also be called, my teacher said. Another *title* for my book! It jolted me, it fixed or secured what I had felt: deviltry and craziness entered whole communities, countries, a time. I felt bad. I valued my mother's letters. They were more *letters* maybe than mine, they had some old trick of letters in just telling what happened over the weekend, yesterday—on Election Day when she and her friends drove to the country house of another friend: a smell of air sharpening over great clear American distances and *thinking*. What smell was that? Air moving and turning the leaves, where, I remembered from my New Jersey grandmother's, lunchtime sunlight in its suspended flow through the porch screens became their glistening surface. I smarted from my mother's phone call. I saw the black pay phone on the wall at the end of the dormitory hall, I went to sleep, knowing her phone calls had been sort of like this *before*.

Then I woke to a day of harsh chance and the blood of the gods (what was its name?) working in me. And *as* I woke I was sweepingly half dream-bound still and proud of some gift of my father's that I had sustained. But how would I know? Why, the weather knew it *for* me—underway with an untroubled tree smell of frost, and harsh in a competitive anarchy of green cloth book bags over the shoulder (making books weapons or mysterious trash) and a geniality in the greetings of "men"—"fresh"-men who often did not know each other.

That day a letter from my mother appeared leaning with shadowy weight in my eye-level post-office box. I would also look *through* that box having once seen an outlandish, pushing fight between two postal clerks, one blond and pink—albino, with a seeming special thickness of eyelash like an impediment of light itself to make things out through—and the other clerk swarthy, grizzled. My mother would have had to write this letter a couple of days at least before last night's call. I value, I wolf her letters and discard them; I could not, no matter what, be bored by her letters, and idly I knew this, and, more than over the phone or in her presence, I saw her sociably changeable face, her undecided eyes, deepening into the present, and had her very voice working in my head when I took into my hand the envelope with the name-and-address imprint in slender red on the envelope and on the same blue-gray stationery inside. But as I opened it, alerted and alarmed, my irritation of last night was dictating the *contents* of this letter I now began to read as if I had already read it.

I read stupidly and slowly and all at once, and took it in. My mother had written the Dean, and she had had a "nice letter" back.

That was what she had had.

A fellow freshman read *his* mail and laughed, he slouched half sideways into a marble window ledge and let out a sort of sequence of short asinine laughs. My mother had written the Dean and she had had a nice letter back. (I was already done, but some mass of me way off center stayed here at the end of these first words about *her* letter and *his* letter as if I were "slow" or stuffed or made lazy by the original *completeness* of an event the words presented me with.) She had thought the Dean might like to see my father's—"your father's"—letter. He had written back that he couldn't agree more, it was a "fine" letter, it had something to say. More people should see this letter.

The Dean, with his absurd shock of white hair, his ruddy, lined stick of a face, his plaid shirt under a brown tweed sports jacket with patches that came around a bit so you could see them from the front, his plaid shirt photographed in the college newspaper on his square-dancing evenings, this *fellow,* this man in an office (but in the country!), had told my mother that he could have the letter printed and mailed to members of her son's class.

Yet his word "could" leaves the decision untaken (unless I am wrong, and I look again to see if the word is "can").

Untaken, though not up in the air.

I wondered that this had happened.

I stood by this comfortable wall of combination-lock post boxes, framed thickly in brass.

I clapped my book shut on the letter and the envelope. The

Dean was not the one who had suggested this, much as I disliked him for it. A chill packed my bowels, a voice of mere sound ran into my head telling me nothing of what to do.

A conversation occurred with a friend from another dormitory late that afternoon. What am I saying? We sat in his room, Paul and I, in his dorm, and enjoyed a conversation— and the freedom to do so, in a society where we presumably belonged. To "visit" with each other, as my grandmother Emmy said.

We droned on, witty, ourselves, free, small, and with long, dense tentacles of reading assignments waiting for us just outside our minds like philosophies of life. Will we make it to dinner or spend our parents' hard-earned money downtown? The only thing Greek about Mike's Restaurant is Mike, according to Paul; is it the décor he's talking about? it's funny the *way* Paul says it, I don't know what I'm laughing at exactly. We're talking about our families in a, for me, reckless fashion. As other *people,* I think. As famous and infamous careers of habit made *up.* My cousins and other relatives are like siblings, I get flip and I get nicely, gently disloyal, I'm going to take this further—and certainly would, no matter what, like a bore.

Though for a while the mystery girl upcountry is under discussion: drinks like a trooper, where does she put it? she never falters for hours on end, according to Paul—*she's* so disgustingly smart *and* funny you would think sometimes that she hasn't time to fuck, but she's crazy, she's nuts: she's wild of course, a year or two ahead of us (he forgets), aren't they always? he'll get her down here yet, some long Sunday afternoon, he'd like to eat her. Has a car but she's stingy with it, he hears. Well, when am I going to *meet* her? I wasn't along the night Paul wangled a car. She's writing a play but it's in poetry, she hates T. S. Eliot, especially his plays, she sees through him, characters all sound the same, she's a very intelligent girl. She's got a couple of friends, *they're* studying *painting.*

When am I going to meet her, when am I going to meet her friends?

Soon.

We drink, satisfied, and express this, helter skelter—throw away our talk upon some moment that then doesn't pass.

PAUL: *You'll* never go to Germany.

I: Next summer.

PAUL: You'll never do it.

I: I want to see those cities before they start rebuilding them.

PAUL: Never happen.

I: Bullshit.

PAUL: That's right.

I: Bullshit.

PAUL: German girls—they just lean their backs up against the wall.

I: Well, you don't want to get rolled.

Is this what Paul's been putting off saying to me? His alarm clock goes off. We don't speak of it as he stops it. It's six *p*.m. He's been getting up early to work.

But now I, with a little preamble—"I've never mentioned this to you, but"—I told him my father was dead. Told Paul, my friend. I had said this. It sounded like my father had died a month ago, or was dead at last.

The possibly stupid sound (even meaning) of the words. At school any number of fools had known. Here no one; two school classmates maybe, who were now my college classmates (if *they* "knew" still). I was embarrassed. What was it? Like revealing that I was on a partial scholarship. When all *this* meant was that I had *earned* a part of my way: though to have to be *given* the money "for your education" meant you didn't have it to start with (which wasn't quite true).

Did my new friend ignore my feeling? Here it was not grief. He said he was sorry. He shook his head. He had a long nose and a long, jutting kind of chin, and eyes cruelly blue, and his quite black, lank hair he restlessly whipped back off his high, narrow forehead. He wanted to know how long my father had been dead. He certainly asked. I almost did not know. "What did your father do?" Paul asked. Again a soothing horror with hands felt in the dark for me, and grief ignorantly stranded me, though in motion.

Then I was embarrassed to have made a moment of it.

I lost face because my father was dead. Of course I did. A secret hue across my torso. Or a name that *some*place I did not keep hidden to my own pointless brain.

In my room I knew his letter by heart. Alone later, I could have broken down and wept wondering what was meant by the German menace: "Winston Churchill pointed to the German menace for years," my father said, "and got only ridicule and vituperation for his pains, but he did not quit in the face of opposition," my father said. *What* opposition? I asked like a troublemaker. His letter had these familiar *phrases*: "Try to take my word for it"—"I earnestly wish you to be a better man than I am."

This was my father, whom I missed. For what? For his attention, but where was it? For his face and body, his wit. And *because he was my father*—the answer a grownup would familiarly give a child. My uncle is my dad's always younger brother and treats me like a most interesting friend. In my ear faraway he says, *Good grief!* and guffaws at his own story. Those words were my father's but it was my uncle I heard. Will I feel older than my father one day?

I *said* the words *"Be a better man"* pressed into anger. A roommate called, "You talking to yourself?" I was where my father had not been—this college, this semiprivate room.

A better man? But my father had lost *his* father at *ten*. Maybe that game was worth letting them have. But why should an investment counselor not die extremely well-off? "Rich," I think, that curiously hard word some friend of my mother's will utter. Arguments were being "pursued" elsewhere, not here. I shouted at my father once, it was like making something up. I hear him, not me. I'm twelve and he says, of my friend (so I know it must be so), "Phil's a debunker, you don't want to be a debunker"; and my father says, "Learning how to get along with people is half the battle"—I yelled at my father, "I *hate* people!"—"*No* you don't!" he shouts back laughing so above it all, so older— and my mind, now at college, has hung on to that piece of my father, hoping for the other half of the battle.

Paul's sitting back deep in his armchair, one leg crossed over the other, lobs a cigarette butt out his window, described people I had not met; and I did that for him.

Pop—*he* came to me now. Why did he take on somebody else's ready-made family? The two boys. The woman. Uneducated, he wished my father to be spared *his* experience. I could have kept him away from my thoughts here in a used room where I was frequently to be found tipping a brown-glass bottle of beer, my eyes steadily on Paul, a friend. Very easy, the two of us, and in the very late afternoon we thought of phoning this girl he knew at the college a half hour's hitchhike away. He had a driver's license, I did not. He said he would phone later, when she would be in.

What did my father *do?*

He wrote a letter. I could not speak of it to Paul, I could not describe my father to him. Then I thought I could, but sometime.

I make a list of people I should write.

Pop could not speak much of my father's death, he would not tell what he had lost, I was sorry for him sometimes. He was my *step*-grandfather. Pop took what action he could. My father's real father through his ancient deadness maintained his mystery, dead of a heart attack in a hotel, the curtain stuck and refusing to fall upon that furnished tableau that "the family" didn't talk about. Not that I had asked them to. Yet a man to me not "young," never mind that my dad was ten. I ran through in my mind what Pop got worked up about. I wasn't sure. I resolved to write him. It would be like talking without him there.

The Dean, so high and resident, was planning with my mother this new printing of the letter. "Lessons in survival," he had presumed to call "things like this." But what did he know about Lincoln, the Lincoln imagined in my father's letter? I wanted to call him up and ask, knowing that he was a professor of economics, and knowing that, what the hell, I was going to let "this" happen. Anyway after that first mailing a year and a half ago it was history.

It is reported to me my father recited the states of the Union in alphabetical order at a party, and in order of admission, and from east to west, and threw in for good measure, since Joe Louis was under discussion, that New Mexico achieved statehood the year it had its one heavyweight championship fight, which Joe Louis was not involved in, by the way, in case anybody was about to ask.

He is quoting someone from the family when he says gleefully that the tomato soup is "as *o* double *t* as *e* double *l*." And when in the course of striving to do a definition of "interdependence" for my loved and feared seventh-grade teacher (she was both of those, and an actual Quaker at the Quaker grade school where I got such high grades my father threatened to move me to "Poly"), I have summoned him to my room as he was on his way out to dinner and he dictates out of his head an airtight definition of that large (gray? blue?) "term" *interdependence* (which sounds very even and right, no need to underline words, *he* says), while my mother's coat rustles with a haste hers *and* its own in the hall by my threshold, and Dad handsomely (and coolly aromatic) stands like my not quite graspable equal (for *I* have contributed ... what? a call upon his knowledge—

he knows mathematics and chemistry without having studied them in years and all current events, and knows that Yiddish sounds like German); while he is given to a possibly terrible but honed reluctance (it's like a modesty, so now I see months after his death that it's my dad's pride grained with *fear*, this sober, but maybe *not* sober reluctance) to believe some vision of the future coming to him while he stood seriously and scented above me.

My father was held to have a command of language. His talk survives in our memory. He punned, he talked history, he says Joe Louis is more than human but not just a machine, my father predicts the round, or we're at a ballgame in the upper deck staring down at Dixie Walker and my father says, He's due for a hit. My father knew French, he loves sports but hasn't the time. He listens so carefully if only he could be present to hear his lawyer-friend who was once at Oxford telling *me* in great eloquent detail how "right" he thought my father's letter was. My father spoke Latin at a party he and my mother went to. He quoted poetry.

And this letter of my father's was written in one *day* quite possibly—two days, a few *hours* (I measured them, but couldn't across the fitted absence of his across every moment in my vicinity)—or he wrote that letter facing a busy week. Why, I'm his brother for a moment. And it wasn't all the feelings my father *had*—I mean that *got into* my father's thinking—only how he was one evening or morning; or after sleeping on it.

It came out one evening, in talk. It got written down. I see him getting it down on paper then while I'm asleep. I have to see the apartment we were in then. Or he knocks on my door during homework time and my room is awash with cigarette smoke, my voice rank, my breath, my nostrils rank and dried, my gums stiff, the cave of my mouth experimental. Nothing is said about it, he doesn't cross my threshold's shallow step. Is my privacy *given* me by him? The letter was dated nearly three years before his death—long before I tried smoking in my room—February twenty-second was the date he put on it—*Washington's* Birthday. Was the letter written *to* me? What about that? (Passed to me in my sleep, a neglected dream, or it made *too* much sense, or made too much of me.) Safely deposited in a bank. Withdrawn to a drawer of the excellent desk in the living room exactly when?

"It" got said to his *friend.* Good. The letter begins with, really, a scene. I can see it at least. My dad's only *referring* to that conversation with Felix: friendly men, they surely helped each other. I didn't "know" "Felix" in the letter—"Mr. Charlton" to me—I did not hear him speaking. I hang on to their names. But the men themselves, who are they here?

"Last night," the letter began, "I got talking to Felix Charlton about the future and how best to prepare our children for it." I checked that week of '43. It's over four years ago, it's gone. The "night" of their talk—"last night"—was Sunday. Because the letter was dated February 22nd. Which was a Monday. Washington's Birthday, a holiday, he wouldn't have gone in to work, that Monday. He wrote the letter after breakfast, after a few morning words with his wife, after reading the *Herald Tribune,* after going to the bathroom—or in the afternoon, when it was raw outside. He could not have said to Felix all that was in the *letter.* He would know what Felix could do for him. Do I mean what I would never? You have to know what you're talking about—but was it either that or *not* knowing?

You know what you're doing, my Poly classmate had said. It didn't always feel like it—maybe that was how "knowing what you're doing" *did* feel. Like not doing quite all you could.

My mother phoned—a ring at the end of the dormitory hall, I was usually right when I guessed it was her calling. It was a couple of nights later, she was having a party. "We're all being very silly," she said, huskily. They were discussing being "on the verge." She named the man who had started it. His voice at once rose in the background, an organist friend of hers. Composer of witty and romantic sacred music, who complained about his disabilities and defeats until everyone's convulsed.

My mother said, huskily, that it was a nice letter from the Dean, wasn't it. I had not seen the Dean's letter, only heard about it—by mail over a distance of a hundred and fifty miles. I listened to her say that it was wonderful what the Dean was doing, he called it an honor.

A door opened down the hall, someone stepped out into the hall and I knew the step. The door closed. I heard no more steps. I said, "It *is* an honor; he's right." I wanted to say, "Bullshit makes the grass grow green"—throw that right in her face. I *love* her.

At my mother's end I heard the guffaw of, I was pretty sure, someone else I knew, and on the piano several strongly declared chords exactly like what they played for the offertory when the wide, shallow, velvety-cloth-lined wooden plates that had been filled up with envelopes, coins, and bills were borne to the front of the church by four men in dark suits.

We're speaking of it, I suppose, this deal with the Dean, it was all but "concluded" I supposed I was being "given to understand." The time approached. I did not ask when the letter was being mailed out; I thought she would not know.

Some fame for the letter would ensue in this place of many people, of future professions, of fact, of future life. Some notoriety for the letter, for the intimate, teaching act of it that would fulfill further our sense of the letter. *Here is what my father did for me.* Was that it? If the letter said more than he said to Felix, his talk with Felix must have made him think.

Was the letter really written to me? My father said, Take my word for it. I think, The officer gives his troops their choice.

Right *now* I'd like to have known my father in college. In the Army Reserve at Harvard just at the end of World War I, photographed in his uniform: "charming," I heard it called: two veins visible along the back of his right hand; the young, rather stunned or emotionless, *posed* face—eyes withdrawn, I guess: a photo "For Aunt Edna," who lived with them with her maiden daughter—"Merry Christmas."

Graduating 1919, war's over, going to work for a chemical firm, helping his family. A while later offered a job in Chicago, much better, turning it down because (my *mother* had told me three or four times) his mother, Emmy, said she could not bear it if he went that far away. One of his Southern cousins, a man a few years younger, said it was that gray-green colorblindness of his that steered this Bachelor of Science out of chemistry; I believed my mother.

Taking at last a job in an investment firm—his family needed help—he could work hard, he was thorough *and* fast, a gentleman-worrier good with figures, with people, one subway stop under the river from the Heights. People said he was the nicest man they ever knew, our dentist said this to me. It was later on the very day we walked out of the counter restaurant in Forest Hills after the intensely quiet tennis matches that my dad said to *me,* "You have to learn to get along with people," and I summoned a stomach-penetrating smell of grease from that grill.

"They were so poor," my mother said to me. His real father was a lawyer. Lawyers were counted among my father's closest friends. His real father had died in a hotel under mysterious circumstances. In college I make them up.

My father dies in an oxygen tent in a hospital, while I am at a church party. The letter is certainly in the desk by then. So he took it from the safe-deposit box, but when? Was it already there Christmas night? The phone rang and it was his mother wanting him to come out, they had our presents, she had not seen him. A winter night, dark with sleet, elements to be battled. He had three weeks to live, but who knew that? My mother said, I don't know why you're doing this. It was Christmas night and she was like an actress, different—quietly unnaturally turned against the moment. It was late as if she were compelled to talk to somebody while playing the violin, when *she* wouldn't talk while playing the *piano*. A bit bitter, an independent person. An awkward conclusion in sight for Christmas day. When he picked up the phone, he was at home with us, comfortable with the day, the evening, the apartment; but when he put it down, he was on his way out to see his mother, who said, "I don't know how many more Christmases I'll be here."

Would the Dean get in touch with me?

The answer, slow in coming, was, Not until next weekend. Life is scarcely to be believed and we have to do something about it.

The Dean dropped me a note typed on college stationery. He sounded like a minister, or I made that up in my collegiate anger. It was a good decision on my part to share the letter. He said it was a fine letter. It was "a good thing to share." Yet did he mean *sharing* was a good thing? It's small of me. I *am* petty. It's a waste. What am I *doing*? I must take his word for it. He said it must help to know how much my father cared about my future. I'm scared.

What did the Dean get out of this? Words came: "a piece of nooky"? "quim pro quo?" I heard the words of my father's letter that weekend and imagined people giving it a look. It should be in the mail Tuesday or Wednesday. I didn't have a copy but I knew the letter pretty well. "A better man than I am." Better *at* something maybe. If so, what? The answer came, but only as voices, faces frowning *and* smiling, not bothering to pooh-pooh my persistence, just dismissing it.

He was "so poor," my mother had said. *He*; not *they*, the family.

Was it true? Was she his angel, walking rapidly, lightly, or in the kitchen making a meal effortlessly, swiftly, "with her left hand"?

I'd just like to have known that fellow, that college freshman. Because I had not lived to know the man he became; or know him better (it came to me sickeningly). To know him half as long as his mother did, or his stepfather, who comes on the scene when my father is ten.

Fresh-faced, somewhat pale-faced fellow, my father at seventeen, my age, in shirtsleeves standing in front of beakers and burners, flames, in a laboratory among advanced odors. Younger than in Aunt Edna's Christmas photo, 1918, where he is in uniform—broad-foreheaded, Irish, if you like; good-looking, family-honoring boy, pale, who will become better-looking still.

Who are those friends he lets take him away from his studies, according to his letter? They talk about how long the war will go on, certainly. He might still be going, he wants to. He has sergeant's chevrons on his Army Reserve uniform in the 1918 photo. The picture extends to just above the knees and the outward fold of breeches where the light catches the ampleness of the heavy cloth along the thigh. In his left hand, barely visible hand, he holds against his leg the stiff, flat brim of his felt hat like what I wore in the Boy Scouts. He is slender, square, I can't tell. What sobering or trivial things is he thinking while the photographer talks and then disappears into the eye of the camera? He looks taller than he is. He isn't frail-looking; but he's got a "leaky valve."

But the war I learn ended a month ago. He plays lacrosse in the spring. It was the crazy game in a way at my school, not at all a hockey-like "spring *football*" (helmets, shoulder pads): lacrosse doesn't pause for the big deal of the *football* field—*plays,* thrill of the season. It's not Wrestling, brainy-punishing and scien*tif*ic, those hand-to-neck-locked leanings and gropings, the pondered pressuring for leverage, then the mind's lunge, the reptile strike (*or* football tackle). Lacrosse I was certain was violently funny. Through masked headgear, faces peer. The bare-legged running up and down a field wields the familiar and

useful-looking "outdoor sportsman's" lacrosse *stick*. Why didn't
I play legendary lacrosse? He was still alive the spring of my
sophomore year in high school, never mentioned it, was content
that I played tennis (never said a word except that it would be
useful to me, but he was dead the spring of my junior year as
I exceeded him in height). Legionary hostilities, lacrosse in truth
some North American hunt. The French got it from the Indians;
the Canadians and English took it from there, dashing around
hacking at one another—as if the ball, rocketingly resilient,
hard-rubber thong-netted in the oval triangle frame at the end
of the shank of the stick were live food on a spring afternoon.

But his chem lab runs late, the long afternoon leaves the
early evening luminous with a leave to do nothing—or something else—to eat, to not go back to the room, to compare
experiences—with someone, anyone but his devoted family, who
are talking of him far away in Brooklyn, sometimes *waiting* for
him.

As long as I was at home, and had them on my trail,
I did well. So well, in fact, that I was given scholarships and was able to go to one of the world's greatest
universities.

With *them on his trail,* he was *able to go.* My thoughts grow
mean. They are on his trail, he will not stop. I follow too,
bleeding the meaning out of him, making it up to haunt him.

He took a tough major, an esoteric, odoriferous major, he
majored in Chemistry at Harvard. They were on his trail.

Where does he eat? I know how, walking, he turns the toe
of each foot a little in as his foot swings forward. What is he
wearing? Will I know him? Would I have wanted to? I want
to know an awful lot of people but do little about it. "... I was
given ..." he says. "I was *able to go* ..." he says. What would

my father at my freshman age have said to let me know the man who could later write the letter to his son?

I don't imagine being him, but he is more important than I am. I am *interested* in him. "I have written all this," the letter said, "because I earnestly wish you to be a better man than I am." And in the Lincoln part, "Yet he got the best out of others by giving the best of himself, and all the time."

Had *I* given his letter to be disseminated by the Dean? *You* know what you're doing, my Poly classmate, the lawyer-to-be, had said. No one else had said that to me, but who *would* have? Was I sustaining his gift? The lawyer-to-be had not seen the letter. But he knew of it (which I had not told my mother). What about the two who had gone on to college "with me"? Would they know? Had they heard about such a letter?

Had the once-admired one known, who'd blackballed me from that Poly fraternity without ever being a member? He had arrived here into a circle of his brother's friends—his taller, beloved brother, seemingly blithe. And he was smart enough to get by; playing poker and bridge, playing percentage, finessing, all night and some days in the dorm next to mine or, more and more, in a fraternity house set back among trees and resembling a suburban home like its white-linteled, brick neighbors—yet a college fraternity was called a "house."

He and I stand outside a classroom door waiting, I'm an immigrant freshman, and he can grin with an awful measure or *tincture* of maturity asking if I can think of our Poly classmate George in a little ashes box who used to play boogie-woogie piano, he's dead in a summertime car crash, getting from June to September.

Our first week, he showed me how to write a check. I don't know why we were in the bank at the same time. How he navigated in full humor and underlying wit, easy vigilance, knew just what the point was—the *connection* between you and him

then and in the light of the rest of his day: he was more so-
phisticated, because he gave expert light conversational attention
when in your presence. I will never hate him. After I wrote the
check, I could do it any time.

The other is Roger, an innocent debater; gifted athlete, he
should have gone to Harvard and played soccer *there*; constantly
(shamelessly) athletic; in a noisy optimistic moral team-sweat; by
temper a frank self-defending strong street-scrapper from somewhere in Brooklyn, of a friendliness quick or noisy; a studious
guy on a scholarship who says how "privileged" he feels, whose
father died years ago and whose mother has always worked.
(Proud of her son—sitting in the kitchen with him—a bit nicely
thin?—alone? Christian. *Pretty,* I imagined, and, thinking as
often before my harbor window of other names for myself, I
tried to know if "Roger" was the name for *him.*)

We have a late-morning class Tuesday and Thursday and I
will sometimes walk to the Post Office with him afterward. I
have foreseen the letter yet not as a Dean's Office envelope
identical to others entering the mailboxes of two hundred and
eighty freshmen. The condemned has ugly surprises on the *way*
to execution. I feel "it" will be "out" before I know it. I looked
for it Wednesday.

Thursday I am slow, I dial my combination as if I am
figuring it out—somebody's near me, and Roger is off by a
window already reading. The Post Office was built with great
inset windows with sills deep enough to write on. We would
lay out our mail there, what there was. The little door came
weightlessly open. I stood there facing my box.

I read the Dean's covering letter feeling safer with *it*. It
praised my father; it accorded him who had not gone to this
college an anonymous celebrity. It did not mention that he was
dead. I felt wide open to those introducing words—"one of your
number." I went then to the letter, unknown because mine. Here
it was further preserved, but it was new (and I was stricken and

encouraged by this). The *words* were different: shrug off such an insight—original with you, maybe your deliverance, but shrug it off. The words of this letter compete with college; I don't want him to have to do this, he is not here to give a full account of himself. My father's second thoughts, third thoughts, partial thoughts. I slip the letter back in the envelope.

The Post Office noised its bareness—or I was exposed—or my mind was my body in that marble-floored—but *is* it marble?—still hopeful building. From one of those large window places Roger, my school and now college classmate, made the first comment that came to me about the newly printed letter from my father.

"Did you get one of these?" I'm addressed by Roger's *voice* somewhat. It reaches me, a crude, exact sound, at once as if I have not already drawn from my box my mail. A postcard, it is mine, with the stamp upside down. Then the long business envelope, a Dean's office address in the upper left. I had seen the albino Post Office employee right through my box. He finds me for a couple of seconds and I have understood a thing that will have to wait. Roger I thought was speaking to me. Why *wouldn't* I "get one of these"?

"What a load of bullshit," Roger says.

My face is conscious of me, we're objective about each other, it and I; and my hand's wrong, as if it's left the envelope; the paper judges me. How fast did he read the letter, or how much of it? Horror happens in me and is inside, lidded. Will I stand for the horror here, of that word? Roger is over there.

Waves are taking over to plunge me down inside me, disaster of the freedom to make up anything at all to say—do—and I think there was more to his first question "Did you get one of these?" and I will, I will, go back to it. The horror is in that voice, which could go on. The letter is my father's letter. *It* has gone on. "The subject is closed," my mother could say with husky solemnness so I feel for her, my *father's* phrase on her lips, her tongue, coming from throat and nose, not from her hands. Or in another room my father, alive this time, is frowning tolerantly. Or working at the desk.

Or, late at night, at the front door in his maroon bathrobe, angry from head to toe, mad, *palely* angry, *hopping* mad, his lips a little pushed out: "What do you *mean* by this?" Judging the soon-to-be fatherless.

If he actually wants an answer, maybe there is none. So he's demanding a change in my—not even my behavior but my *body* it comes to me now in college, this night that I came home after midnight, it is Christmas vacation, there *is* no answer, *Christmas Vacation* hollos through my unwary head, it has at this moment *all gone wrong,* every bit of it, every hope of it, this night kissing not the one I loved but a girl I hardly knew—until I stopped wondering when her mother would come home, the girl's hand on me, my face, my collarbone—and then *talking* about it, she and I, about kissing, about a double-fluted curve she almost like a sister makes her tongue do again now to show me what I have just been *feeling* as the clock passed midnight and twelve-fifteen, knowing that luckily tonight I'm a two-minute run from home, and kissing until one a.m., wanting to hold one of her stocking feet when she drew it up and her knee lifted her skirt, but all erased by my father's anger at the door, intimacy exploded inside out. And yet it was *interestingly* scary and remembered in bed early Sunday morning when I heard the front door and my father padding back along the hall, the paper in his arms, reading the top half of the front page, peeling back a section or two, I knew.

I would not stand there with Roger in the Post Office, it was horror that he did not find the letter Excellent. I was "mortified." Let *him* be stuck with things *he* knew. A father he hadn't known. Or one he really had.

"A load of bullshit": I'm mortified, stuck: aren't I? I weighed the waiting that I'd understood I'd have to bear, and like Roger my father could say what he damn pleased, this all could be *discussed*: but this isn't quite it, and will have to wait, this further truth that's with me (and *I* know I'll track down if I have to) must wait still to *come* true: "bullshit": I felt my poor father at the desk, "a load of bullshit," in bed writing on a yellow pad, its cardboard backing against his raised knees, asking me at six in the afternoon, Christmas vacation, what I had "made" of it, "the" *Hamlet* he'd arranged for me to see with the out-of-town son of an old friend of his who knew more than I; and I didn't tell my father, sitting up in bed at near suppertime on a Saturday of Christmas vacation with a book on the blanket called *Two Years Before the Mast* (my mother arriving with two glasses of sherry) and maybe the Letter by now moved from the safe deposit to the desk drawer, that the star's saliva (as someone sitting behind me said so *I* then saw it) had showered fascinatingly like light in the footlights arcing upon the front rows. But it was the acting I could mention, the things done that I saw, the words came and went, came back again while here in the Post Office I daydreamed and, as at church, knew that I must do something but that if I didn't, nothing was going to happen.

Roger in the Post Office: I both was and was not thinking that Roger's father had died years before mine. I would not stand there with him, this insulting competitor I would not argue with—"scholarship guy"—and as I locomote steplessly toward the next windowsill, I can read what's in the already slit-open envelope. It looked good. Paper crackled near me. Roger's letter was gone in the waste bin.

"I'll have to read it later," he heard me say.

"What a load of bullshit," Roger said, as he passed me without asking where I was going. What *had* he been reading? What lines, what thoughts?

This in the small town of that soon-to-be-snowy college. I had spoken the name of this college quite arbitrarily one evening urged with oddly jolly respect by my mother and an Irish businessman-singer friend of hers to divulge my first choice. I said it with a little rising sound of decision—wasn't it *ob*vious?—as if to create suspense in retrospect—keeping my own counsel, feeling a little silly yet not wanting to hurt *their* light jollity. Or let *it* jolly *me*. I had chosen this one after weeks of mentioning three or four colleges and living in some connection of myself with each of their *names*. Of this one I seemed to feel more after my threateningly quiet announcement. A *small* college, where I would be known to my teachers and to others. And not to the mountain nearby, which *I* would come to know.

I did not know where to go, where to move myself. Fifteen minutes later I ascended the Post Office steps again. I opened and closed my mail box and I went to a broad windowsill and read the faintly fragrant postcard from the dark-haired girl in Brooklyn Heights, the ink dark-pink, the stamp upside down, the message *knew you'd look* palpably beneath the half-licked stamp. But I had an eye on the post boxes. I unfolded my father's letter and I read it.

"Bullshit" was the wrong *word* for my father's seriousness, for that tone of careful explanation (though here not playful— would he play at explaining? he could, yes, but not the day he wrote these words):

> In retrospect I am appalled by my neglect of the vistas which life has opened to me. Both Mother and Dad were firmly convinced that a college education was the principal requisite of success. They never let me forget about it, nor did they fail to impress upon me constantly that they were financially unable to send me to college, and that therefore I must achieve this objective by my own efforts. As long as I was at home, and had them on my trail, I did well.

A freshman I knew only to nod to in rough agreement on the street, a stubbled fellow who was on the freshman football team, tried to lift the flap of the envelope without tearing it, the Dean's secretary had not licked it well perhaps. He was reading my father's letter, he lowered his eyebrows. The fellow he was with who I was pretty sure wasn't a freshman, waited. The one I knew left off, turned to the end, read it, and handed the letter to his friend. Now *he* read it. Then they looked at each other, that was all, two big guys.

A friend of mine who was in a hurry pulled out his mail and lost it, dropped it all. He looked down at it there on the marble floor. He seemed to come to a decision and bent to gather it up. My friend Paul came by with two freshmen, one his roommate. He stopped to tell me one of his apropos-of-nothing jokes. He went to his box.

I hope he likes the letter. Is it propaganda?

He withdrew three envelopes. He was talking and he stuck his mail in his jacket pocket. It was fearfully final and needed— the Post Office; the divided volume of mail; unholy daylight nourishing my new home, and some awful thing I must do in the vicinity of others. I asked Paul if he'd gotten anything good; he showed me the envelopes, "Tell you later"—was I having lunch? He turned to speak to someone as I shook my head; it wasn't quite that he didn't care if I was having lunch, it was like my father's "leaky valve," his heart murmur when I had spoken of it to Paul, who made it up as he went along, my lunch plans were of limited interest to others (it came to me), or taken for granted like a ride up to that girls' college this evening, or its postponement until tomorrow which was always possible. A woman with silver-blond hair came slowly and beautifully past me, reading my father's letter—the wife of the college *chaplain*!

I looked into the New England waste bin nearest me. It was filling up and I reached in and got my hand around my father's letter at once. I opened it out and it had a finger or thumb print in the lower corner quite dark, once moist perhaps. I reached back in and turned over assorted envelopes, a brochure, a post-card, a bank statement from Boston with, across a top corner, "Please take care of this" in back-slanting longhand in cinna-mon-colored ink.

There was Roger's letter; it moved when my eye found it, it was a scrunch, not a crushed ball; I opened out the two cor-rugated pages. What *did* he read? Maybe not the same thing as the chaplain's wife. Her unlipsticked mouth had been pursed, her tan skin wholehearted, a serious or alert person capable, I believed, of abrupt laughter. She liked the letter. She's engrossed by it. I wanted to tap her lightly on the shoulder.

"Throw away a check?" a man asked behind me, an elderly, an *old,* man. He wore a greenish jacket like nothing I had ever seen, with narrow panels of the same tweed cloth down the front seemingly attached with extra buttons. It seemed a time for humor or politeness and I thanked him. I didn't think so, I said. He said, "Let me know if you find anything." I wanted to show him the letter, ask him what he thought. Was it written at a sitting?

I had four copies. A fellow was drawing his mail out and opening each envelope before taking the next one out of his box. He looked my way scowling. He came toward where I was, he walked upright measuredly as if he were stiff-legged, I had seen him before, he wore a jacket and tie with a military stripe, he stopped right next to me, he was a freshman because he was reading my father's letter. He went on to the second page. I *had* seen him before. He read fast and thoroughly.

But *what* mysterious thing must I do? It existed. It was in me, I saw. Despite the many months, I must do it at once. The fellow standing surly or stern almost elbow to elbow with me returned to the first page and read for a moment. Then he addressed me by my last name—"That's your name?" I looked at him blankly. After a moment I nodded. It was a thing I did.

"What do you think of this letter?" he said; "have you read

it?" I envisioned a democratic consultation headed my way, a sternness, some latent intellectual outrage there. He was going to force some issue of the letter upon *me*. "You've read this letter," he said undeniably.

"But did you read the Dean's?" I said dryly.

"*His* letter?" the fellow said.

"I could break his neck," I said warmly, happily. "Come to think of it, I really could. I wonder how this happened," I said.

"I take it at face value, the father's letter," the fellow said.

I gestured with my hand that held the Dean's printed pages—"What is it, did you come here to get more of this parental crap?"

"Why yes," he said, but had surprised himself. "*You* consider it that?"

"No I don't, but I don't know what I think," I said. Yet felt I was in college and being given new chances. "I mean you'd have to know who this guy was," I said.

"*'Was'*?" my classmate asked.

"I mean did he want to be Lincoln?" I said rashly. "Did he want to be Churchill?" I could see my father walking with Mary Todd Lincoln but couldn't see him with a beard, I could see myself with one but not him. And could see myself with her, and him in his uniform.

"I don't get that at all. I don't know about you, but I think this is pretty good advice," my classmate said. He looked me politely in the eye, he might be irritated. "We might talk about this with others who have read it. Shall we do that?"

"Who would be interested in doing that?" I said.

He introduced himself, his name was Manning. As he turned away, he paused. He indicated the letters in my hand. "You have extra copies." I nodded. He shrugged with forthright humility. He asked what dorm I was in; he would be in touch with me. He departed.

He said no more than he needed. But that was not my way,

I saw. And yet if I thought of myself as often saying too much, of my family saying this of me, I had also said nothing: for where had been my words? Had I wanted the letter to go out, had I wanted of all people my mother and the Dean to do a deed I could have vetoed? This fellow Manning was formal, not *older* so much as touched by the *presence* of old people. But were old people this serious? No. He's *naïve*, that's it—or's been brought up in unusual sobriety.

My father's letter? I had sort of forgotten it. But they're *my* words, mine now. Out on the street I saw the Dean, a happy man, a power disguised as someone vivid whom I could go ahead and imagine, that politician's white hair (I'm writing a paper on the filibuster!), a lunchtime celebrity greeting others with an unvarying sincerity weird and weirdly familiar—

I know from my own personal observation that an av-
erage man who persists and works hard is much more
likely to accomplish something worthwhile than—

other folk instantly known to him, faculty, students, some *I* knew, the Jewish proprietor of the laundry and cleaning estab-lishment, the chaplain's wife (whom the Dean kissed on the blatantly brand-new fall stage of this stupidly bright day, for I wondered if college was a place where I could just ask her about that letter she had been reading). I have four copies on me, but the Dean, who's introducing my father to my classmates, won't see me.

I was wild and wastefully excited, walking that village street, the bookstore, the hardware store that did radio repair, the clothing and athletic-goods store, two restaurants side by side, "greasy spoons" they were called by my father.

A terrible memory came upon me. His words are my words too. I give them back, if not to him. He shares his learning with his friend from Oxford, the formal man. He shares himself also with those with whom he and my mother can be "silly." I've had my supper and have come out again to play. The street is soft and at every moment swiftly waiting to my feet, and the motion of my shoulders and arm throwing is just as much my environment as the easy quiet of a friend and his sister I'm having a catch with. I see him coming home late, down our block, my dad, his newspaper under his arm folded not to the front page but the page he was reading when his subway train reached the first stop in Brooklyn. From our group I call across the street, "Drunk again, Dad?"

I have called those words across the street, and a moment later he summons me to join him and we go in.

What did he say? I've lost all but the sense, maybe that too. He did not say No to my meaningless question called in the street. You didn't say things like that, he said. I could stay in, he said.

Where did *my* insulting words come from? the movies? no place? the Bible? Then echoing *his* words or mind? He had very good manners. He could be in me. I will understand this for myself. I will not ask somebody who would not understand. Could the letter be described as a "hardly immortal" letter? Would *any* father have written such a letter? But what *would* a man be able to do, in the absence fixed by his death? I couldn't think. Did I have to? What if there were no copies left? Cells were said to replace themselves. Did they know how? I looked across the street and knew for a second all that was in me. Bring on the letter! My father isn't on any mission. *Could* someone else have typed it for him? He gave me a typewriter for my eighth birthday in a summer house in Massachusetts where I stuffed twelve frogs into a jar and left it on the soft grass in the sun— as an *experiment* (for I didn't have an aim, only the knowledge of curiosity). But the machine arrived on the train and as he got down the last steep step my father handed the heavy but not really heavy black case like luggage to me to carry to the car and kissed me. My mother is between us and the car and I bore in my hand at the end of my straight arm the hard black new case containing the typewriter I wouldn't receive until tomorrow.

He left behind him also insurance, he left some stocks, books, a bolt of gray-blue worsted material in the blanket chest, a gold watch, mainly things he shared with my mother. (He left *sentiment*!) The books belonged more to the apartment, except for his much-written-in Bible; you could "take" them if you wanted. He left his clothes in the closet (and never came back from the hospital). Took his shaving brush and wooden-dished shaving soap grained in arcs like some painting or a partly used cheese or some margarine. He left my mother, he left friends who I believed cared for me, liked talking with me.

I had a ride up to the girls' college if I wanted that evening probably. I had charged two of the new long-play records at the clothing store, which sold records. A charge account. They agreed I would walk out with these LPs. I was contaminated by a "lunchtime" betrayal of my father that was also "nothing." I waved to someone as I crossed the street—one of my friendly roommates, I saluted him, I was going to my dorm, to my room. I smelled rolls. My father's letter was being shared again. Did I want not to hear stupid things *openly* said about it? Was it a written part of an unwritten will? Furnished me before I'd thought of asking for it.

I had time. I had room in which to do something. It was my mother's doing, and before her "the family's." Hunger spurred some plan. Still, I had *no* time—if "the thing I must do" was in response to the letter being all over the place. The words were in those sentences of his. I passed the administration building, its eyelike brick arch softening its old front. I reached a fraternity house, with down ahead on my right the library. Some words as I turned onto a path toward the freshman dorms reminded me I had already lived many years.

Laziness consists primarily of not doing what one ought to do when one ought to do it. I enjoyed loafing and could easily be persuaded to loaf. I knew that I could slight my work and still get by.

But I would leave his words behind me in this fall air which I could live off. Brittle leaves above me, I fingered bark and did not know the tree.

. . . I did well. So well, in fact, that I was given scholarships and was able to go to one of the world's greatest universities. After I got there, I gradually got diverted by trivial things.

A Bible chapter I have by heart says *when I became a man I put away childish things.* For I had to know it when I joined the church. I had enjoyed its writing, which possessed a fullness and an after-sound when spoken by me, in private. "Childish" was different from "trivial." I've read an essay on daydreaming by James Thurber, the cartoonist, and he said daydreaming was O.K.; I read it in the library. And in my Poly Sci book I found my New Testament chapter quoted; then, as if all because I happened to know that chapter, I had actually heard a teacher say—seen him say—and say lightly—"I am become as sounding brass, or a tinkling cymbal," so that if you didn't know the passage, you wouldn't know if the words were his. *I* know. But do I know the thing that pointlessly in the Post Office I sensed "could wait"?

You could go upon what you were yet to know. It was the early afternoon, the truant time. The mountain dark green and here and there a flat dusk color and a patch of orange or rusty gold. It was partly what I was paying for. Those who knew it called it The Dome, and you could go and stand in front of a building with classical pillars and a long triangle pediment and see The Dome green beyond it. I carried my new LP records. I had a class at two, the four copies of the new letter filled subtly the inside pocket of my jacket, Roger's copy crunched, reopened-out, and refolded among the others. I've got to play my records. I need to eat. But there's nothing to speak of to eat where I'm going.

My new LPs under my arm, I turned away and took a different way back downtown, it was all wrong, I ought to have left the records in my room—on top of my roommate's portable phonograph—gone to a dining hall where I took most of my meals paid for by the month, I ought possibly to have done very little. I was hungry. Only let the letter be not dull!

I passed the restaurant I liked—the Greek's. I picked up the steel snap-knock of the pinball launcher, the crack of bumpers. I breathed grease cooking, meat grease, bacon grease, bacon, an onion sweetness of meatloaf to overwhelm time and the waste of time—and hot coffee, a comfort of cigarette smoke, the air of pitcher beer sitting, a wheaty after-spread of Breakfast Out. A phone rang inside among the noises. I had heard my friend Paul say the only thing Greek about the place was the owner. Why would the chaplain's wife get mail in a post box downtown?

I walked clear to the Post Office. Its low-rising steps were easy flying, but you almost weren't getting anywhere. At the counter the sullen albino weighs manila envelopes one by one for a woman with wide shoulders. I scout the waste bins and there it is, scrunched yet balled, page 2 of my father's letter in that grab-bag shit can of crisp papers. Has an impression been made on this copy? Why did the letter get from the safe-deposit box in the basement of a Wall Street bank to the living-room desk?

What if I retrieve all but a few of the letters? But what if my father's letter apart from the paper it's printed on adheres to the sweated brain cells of some freshman who did not have much in the way of mail? Manning liked it; Manning understood it—more than I did, maybe!—maybe loved it. Somebody else comes to mind—one of my roommates or Paul or the chaplain's wife. Or someone who found the Dean's Office envelope *unopened*!—in the basket—and opened it—and now knows some of my father's words—will *have* them as if he's known them all along.

Will the letter follow me all the days of my life multiplied for each occasion? No. I want my mother to know about this, just to *know*. I will talk, no matter what.

Some few among the two hundred and eighty had shown the letter to their friends. For a momentary *reason*, too. The football player handed it to his friend. I rooted in the day's postal waste: here's just what my dad, who's there ahead of me, warns against in the letter, trivial things like when did the letter move from a safe-deposit box to our living-room desk? It was withdrawn from the bank. I am where he was not. This college, this body. This stomach.

I don't have to seek nooks. His gentleness unwaveringly helps, I grasp now—as if I'm looking into him meanly. A goodness you don't argue with. Also *less* than good! Thoughts burst, like fun or a chance—*do* burst (and I won't be told that they do not): he was too good, for example, and gave himself away, my mother said, had the nerve to want *me* to do what he had *not* done (and I won't be told he didn't) so he could only guess at it. He showed himself naked a lot drying himself, dusting talcum down his pale stomach down onto the hairs like light, the light quite living—it just goes into air and is more than he, as if I can see him shimmering as just one inhabitant of the earth.

I see that that is what I want this afternoon magnetized by the mail, detoured round class, food, new people, that he *be* a mere inhabitant of earth.

It's a relief in my busy solitude that had better be of impending decision. Then the relief goes away leaving its shape full of ruin and a future one day or so long in its unfigurable hunger. What have I done? But the letter left out things—more than things.

From one teacher we learned that the century had thought too much. I wrote it down. Someone else actually had said this but I was quite sure the teacher, whose class I had not forgotten I had this afternoon, agreed. These gentlemen in their jackets talked of centuries. We learned that one had to *decide* to think. *Did* we learn?

I make such a decision—like enlisting—and feel ignorantly obliged. Like I'll probably get my head handed to me. Push it further: that my father's death left too many things unsaid. Too many for him? I speak for others, I can't not. Would they be interested? I was shot through with things unsaid.

V

The chaplain's wife has a thick sandwich in her hands and she notices me through the restaurant window. She looks at me over her bulging bread, keeps looking and then eats, she's at the round table in the window, she's with her husband and someone I have seen. Then I'm *in* side, and Paul and the senior who runs the college radio station are vacating a booth; Paul calls me, but I'm near *her,* the big street window before me, and I have spoken and will know what stilted or absurd thing I have said to her whom I don't know only by what *she* says in *reply.* Her husband's frowning and beaming up at me, the fellow with them is an apparently emaciated member of my class I've seen a couple of times hurrying along to keep up with a gigantic, ferocious bald man who teaches Biology and is in the lab all day and all night from what I have heard.

"I felt, I felt," she is saying; but she can't say what it was. "I'll read it again, I want my girls to see it. What did *you* think of it? that's what *I'd* like to hear."

"But he wanted to know what *you* thought, he wanted *you* to say," the emaciated freshman lit into her.

"Oh *shut* up, Tommy," said her genial husband.

The woman began again, her face was alive with friendly tension: "I felt, I felt inspired, I felt . . ." she shook her head smiling, knowing. "There's a secret in there, though. *You've* sensed it," she said. I was flattered.

I said, "I hate people." My classmate grins up at me. The pinball keeps beeping. I hear my name behind me. "That's half the battle," he gloats. "Listen, you don't just *mail* a letter like that," he said.

"It wasn't meant to be mailed. The Dean explained that it was left after the man died," I said.

"Wasn't that moving," the woman affirmed.

"It was meant for his friends," my classmate said with quiet absoluteness.

"It made me mad," I said.

"How so?" the chaplain said—for about the five hundredth time in his life.

"It was the secret in there, wasn't it," affirmed his wife. "I kept taking it out of my bag to look at it—right in the street." She ran her tongue over her lips and wiped her mouth with her paper napkin. She held her sandwich, the finger and thumb of her other hand pinching the handle of her coffee cup. Her blond, silvery hair flowed to her shoulders. Her tan speaks *for* her. Her breasts lurk happily in the heavy, complex knit of her sweater, the wool.

"I thought he was just saying how he felt the day he wrote it. He wanted his son to—you don't know who it is, do you?" I asked the chaplain.

His wife said, "What's *he* thinking right now?" She took a slow, careful bite from that sandwich, which, overflowing, looked like tunafish salad.

"Why would he want a whole lot of people reading that letter?" I said.

The chaplain puts his hand up to me, it's cupped, he says his name. I take his hand, straightening it out, and say mine. Is this college somewhere you just join a table of strangers? There's a folded document sticking out of his jacket pocket and he presses his hand against it looking up at me, and he's not smiling: "I've only had a chance to glance at it."

"It makes you think," I say. "I mean about what to do with your life." I nearly quote the letter. "I mean he has all these regrets, looking back. What he went into."

"I don't recall what he went into," says the chaplain.

"*Went into?* Oh, it's probably there," chimes in my emaciated classmate resigned.

"I'm not sure it is," says the woman. She's looking up at me very seriously, with love.

The emaciated one asked what *my* father was in, but the chaplain said what had *that* got to do with the price of eggs, but I said, slowly, that he was in government service. "That's all you're going to say, it's sort of secret," said my rival, hearing my hesitation and asking for a punch on the nose and knowing there was a place and time for it. I said all this was interesting anyway and it was nice talking to them. I bowed ever so slightly, all but hearing the music of my new LPs coming up through my hand and arm. The chaplain said that one could read it every five years and it would mean something different, but his wife said, "Oh Edward," and gave me a wonderfully unsmiling look returning mine as I turned with objectivity and ease away.

I had breakfast at the counter. Paul and the big wheel had gone. The minute hand on the clock over the jukebox jumped a notch. I had not asked those people for what I wanted but I had gotten it almost. I had not quoted the letter:

> I do not for a moment deny that there are such things as lucky breaks. Or that some people are quicker mentally than others just as some can run faster than others. But I do say that luck will not carry a man through life. . . .

It wasn't the slickest writing—"not for a *moment*"? really?—but it was his. Cup in hand I swung around on my stool but did not see a copy of the letter anywhere among the booths. For an instant, a moment, the chaplain's wife at the far end by the window caught my eye, or I hers. I had not said where I had seen her reading it, but she had implied the street. I wanted to tell her I had called out, "Drunk again, Dad?" I wanted to tell her how my grandmother had said to him this might be her last Christmas. I wanted to tell how I sometimes imagined where he was. It might be possible. The letter moved before my eyes with each person who laid eyes on it. I wanted to ask her when *she* thought it had been moved from the safe deposit across the river to the living-room desk. No, I wanted to ask that skinny little bastard *with* them. I had made them speak.

The radio-station guy was the one with the car. Paul wasn't at the pay phone, which he seemed to use when he came here. I had not turned in his direction while I was talking to the three in the window. Paul was in my afternoon class, if I went. The minute hand lurched upward; "*I'm* looking *o*ver a *four*-leaf *clo*-ver" was chorusing out of the jukebox. Someone poured beer out of a pitcher from two feet above the glass.

I questioned the family and my mother. I could hear their surprised, slow voices answer in their turn that they were sorry I felt that way. They had had no idea. I heard their way of speaking: "One thing at a time"; "a fine man"; "wonderful letter"; "I've always said" (but *I* have *not* always said—not to *them*—not even now, secretly). I could hear their minds resent mine. The "women"—I thought of them like that—had never seriously disagreed with anything I had just up and said. I felt Pop's tight little arm sinews, and the back of my legs as he told me to walk with a spring in my step walking down from the house to the lake, don't walk flat-footed. On the cruise my grandmother and step-grandfather took once, he won all the deck-tennis matches. My questioning of these people went on; it didn't count.

"What about tonight?" I'm asking Paul, as the second-floor

class bell clangs alive above us. He's for some reason standing alone, I'm just in time. "Didn't you hear me at Mike's?" he demands. "I spoke to you three times. That woman plays a very good game of tennis, the chaplain's wife, so does he. She's a rock climber, I'd like to fuck her. Listen, I may have a car and then again I may not." "It's Existential," I reply. But he seems to crane his neck looking to the other end of the corridor as if he'll find a car leaving for the girls' college to the north. "Take good notes for me. I'll see you later, I have to go," Paul said. He went away, I thought of calling him to take my records to my dorm, he didn't have my room key; he ducked down the stairs.

I'm asking someone in the seat on my left if he got that letter the Dean sent out; but he hasn't been to the P.O. today. "Yeah, what was that all about?" the guy in front of me says over his shoulder, as if he's being friendly. But the voice, the professor-soul we overhear three times a week, is at work again, the roll not called but possibly sounded in that large ruminating brain.

If I'm doing *what* I'm supposed to be doing *when* I am supposed to be doing it, where am I this hour? My father's "crowning failing"? It didn't sound right. Is the letter losing itself in my memory? What was the thing I must do, that came to me in the Post Office? But I belong here, and I write it down: *I belong here.* The fellow on my right glances at my notebook, I feel.

My cruelty is overwhelming: "Why *did* you make him come out and see you that Christmas night when he wasn't feeling well?" It rises out of control like the very best vengeance expanding my head.

The wandering voice inside this room speaks of wild ducks in a pond—where?—in a park, and speaks German words without translating them. Paul didn't get to tell me his reaction. It's early to be checking dorm wastebaskets. I snicker at myself, the dorm wastebaskets. The fellow on my right nods a few times and glances my way, he heard me and agreed. I write the German down, *Die Juden sind unseres unglück*, as the voice now gives us the English, somehow I know how to spell the German. The voice asks what is our misfortune, the voice asks what it means to speak for one*self*, and if it means to speak for others, the voice goes on unchecked to inquire if the *silence* of *not* speaking for oneself could ever *express* silence for *others*.

My neighbor observes what my pen writes: *A brother to compare notes with*. His head twitches in my direction back and forth as he writes.

I see for a second on the notebook page before him, *I belong here*. I see *Die Juden sind unseres unglück*.

The voice keeps asking and keeps answering, asking and answering its disturbing questions: its way of carrying on takes my mind off what to do about the letter. So does tonight. Who here is bent upon getting laid tonight? I think, and who from here to the mountain, and who already on the road north?

I'm going *with* my father Christmas night: at the curb I'm shooting out my hand, my finger, my angry loyalty, for a cab; whereupon the sleet turns to rain and lets up. But *I* am *not* going with him, I'm staying home like my mother. But I hit upon a reason for *him* to not go out and see "the family" tonight and he is persuaded by me. He's grateful, witty, living. I know he hopes that I get all A's at the end of the next marking period at the end of January.

But yet another call comes; and though he exchanges greetings, it is no Christmas call: "You believe I can persuade them," he goes on ... "Indeed it *would* be," he replies ... "Yes," he replies after a moment, "Yes, on everyone concerned," he says—and, presently, "Say it again," after which he listens for some moments before hanging up. Who wants something *this* time? my mother asks. It is his country that's calling on him, I know—

although he says to her, "Just business"—in fact, he would have *missed* this call, I see, if I had not persuaded him with a wisely surprising reason not to set out on that trip through naked wind and sleet and the waning of December 25th to make it a real Christmas for his mother. *What* wisely surprising reason? I can't think. I look all over this classroom and see no letter, no Dean's envelope. Yet the letter has changed more than one soul here surely, anonymous, not "Letter from ——— to his son" this time, just "Dear ———." Some ass in the front row asks an insincere question regarding the freedom of the will and is ignored. His extermination is not called for, though I let life suck blood from his dumb neck where there's a brown leaflike birthmark. A thought bleeds: it's that my father *wanted* to see them on Christmas; his mother knew this. (They're whole-hearted.) It was *his* life, it had gone on for many years, after all, and he was maybe seeing what would *happen*. My mother really didn't care to go out there herself.

My name has been called in the classroom, my improbable sound becomes necessary and improbable—a roll of one name!—interrogator-soul can see that I'm present surely—and it's my move but I can't divulge the identity of the letter writer and that I'm aghast and proud, it's here sticking out among us more even than if his name had been on the letter—which the Dean could have done at the risk of his life and reputation—that advice about doing *what* you're supposed to do *when* you're supposed to be doing it may grow in mystery and menace given the rueful anonymity of our adviser my dad if I can only keep it to myself when I answer a question whatever it was: "It's a case of thinking ... and saying and *knowing* ... that, well, 'I belong here,'" I said out loud to a subtle hush in the room. It's a finesse, the simpleness, the all-purposeness of my answer, I didn't hear what was asked.

The professor-soul resumes, surprised to be taken aback,

goes on, alive, probably profound, but I want to make a fool of myself, a nuisance in the *manner* anyway of an assassin. Until the bell clangs outside.

I am complimented silently (and silenced) by persons around me. I'm leaving the room, when the face of the teacher, now nearly profiled, dies, the jaw hangs, blotches teem and crawl and somebody named Rush who tilts his head as he speaks stops me with a grin, though we remain in motion: "Hey, he wasn't looking for anyone to *answer* that question, you really stopped him." "But he called my name." "He what? What do you mean?" Rush passes on out the door, it doesn't matter, he tilts his head to speak to somebody. The professor-soul's question now comes to me: it was about how we are to judge the reaction of German Jews to the rise of anti-Jewish sentiment. And my name was *not* called; no, he was only looking at me.

But I catch two of them up outside. One is the fellow Rush who I happen to know has soccer practice; the other is a troublesome-looking sharpshooter who stops and flips a cigarette up into his lips. Rush tells me our professor-soul gives good notes; his friend stops and lights his lighter a number of times before he puts the flame to his cigarette. I'm asking if they got their mail today; neither replies for some reason. You get things in the mail, naturally, and you could be held responsible. "I got this thing from the Dean; we all did."

The fellow with the cigarette instantly says, "I think it was made up. Nobody would let his father's letter be used like that." It seemed as far away in his words as a Post Office wastebasket. "Oh no," says Rush with manly softness or geniality, "no," he says, "plenty of reasons, *beaucoup* reasons." "Plenty of nonexistent ones," his friend replies.

"He just let it happen," I explain.

"Right, as usual, eh what?" says the fellow with the cigarette surprisingly—"Hey, what do you mean he called your *name?*" he demands, though it's Rush I've spoken about this to.

"He didn't *have* to," I said. "He didn't have to call my name."

"You can say that again."

I say, "So *who* made it up, if it's made up?"

"Whoever wrote it," my man argues glumly as if not smart. Let them go their way.

"He probably wanted to unload it," I'm saying.

"Onto you" is what I hear, and a live butt lands in the grass near the path by my foot. I feel my father's thoughtful, thorough smile in the muscles of my own. Does the guy want an argument or to get pasted one?

Let them go their way, all of them. I saw rooms, a letter in every room. I want to invisibly know, I want to hear my father praised, it's humiliating he's dead but I don't want him here, I have to do something about it but it's too soon *and* too late.

I'm climbing stairs, but I am different now, my mother and father aren't here, I don't have to do a thing, I am at home in the Quad, in any freshman dorm, I don't have to be anywhere, my mother hates me, she wants what is best for me, I love her and she loves me. I'm in a room with a desk exactly like mine, I don't care if someone comes in. Books line up along the windowsill, an envelope sticking out of one which I go and pull an inch or two up, it has a name and address in longhand in the left corner. There is no letter in this room, I know it.

Dorm sounds separate, they're easy. Another door is locked and a voice calls from within, I go on. I'm in another unlocked room with three one-dollar bills gray on a red blanket at the foot of the bed. I dawdle at a window, wondering exactly what the girls Paul's acquainted with are *like,* I have to remember not to give my full name right off, girls don't like that. People who live in these rooms haven't had time to leave my father's letter here yet, they're carrying it with them.

I sit in someone's chair, my LPs on my knees. They have no right to my father's letter. I close a door responsibly. I go by open doorways, typewriters, book-silled windows light and lone through doorways. I have looked into three suites in a row, three rooms in each, letters correspond to people not rooms. I see just one letter. It's on a desk, it's centered opened out upon a green blotter with leather corners. It's waiting, midafternoon getting later. Whose is it? Where is the envelope? My father could call me.

I stand outside in the Quad for some minutes by an Entry reading a record jacket to keep my eyes down, aware of trees, beauty, someone in glasses passing.

I'm on the stairs again, it's not my dorm, I turn the knob of Paul's door. He's got the middle room, two unopened-looking envelopes lie on his desk, I call him and a roommate of his calls my name out of sight: "He *was* here." "Tell him I was looking for him, about tonight. It's all set, I guess." I know Paul's copy of my father's letter is here somewhere, I stay here in the central room, Paul's, I want to ask what this Czech roommate of Paul's thought about the letter. He's swarthy, with an English accent, "Lend-Lease" Paul calls him, he has very grooved tennis shots, stiff and stocky-looking tennis shots, he's cocky on the court, noisy, good; he speaks German with the other roommate, who took it in high school; but he has to study, he's busy, I can tell from how he speaks to me from his room rather intentionally as if his words might fade out: the women *were* coming *here* but the one who was supposed to phone didn't, and Paul only had a ride *up* there so he's hoping he can get her to come down *here,* she has a car or something, or drive *him* down here if he finds her up there. I said I had some unfinished business with Paul and I thought he would be staying here. "Check," the roommate affirms, but I know he will remember what I have surprised myself saying.

I'm down the hall once more, knocking; one door's locked, the next isn't. Why am I doing a thing that's dumb, wasteful— it's showy to my*self*! An August football magazine with the college predictions has my father's letter in the Dean's envelope, it doesn't belong to me, I hate its owner, I am so sorry for him and I see him hurt, I open the letter, and it's the second page on top. I'm happy, intensely economical, occupied. I'm reading the words: "Hard work is really a measure of determination . . ."; and "he was confronted by corruption among the many who were interested in making money for themselves rather than winning the war." I turn back, in some new order: "dream of a rapid and easy climb to affluence and influence . . ."; "hope that a wished-for result will come about by itself, with little or no aid from me or effort on my part."

But what in the world did my father *ever* hope would come about by itself without his doing something? He worried himself to death, my mother remarks. My heart is hitting both sides of my ribs, two hearts? why not? I've never seen mine. This main middle room, small rooms to either side of it, smells of cigarettes, they all do, but the window's open, the mountain stands there. For Christmas, what did he want?

What's left of him here in this place? Some limb, my hand with fingernails. I come and go like any dormitory dweller. The next floor's familiar, I don't live here. Each letter's becoming different, it's the person who's laid eyes on it.

My *father* had changed. I was sure of it, he had become a little lazy through the dissemination of these words, "aid *or* effort," "affluence *and* influence"! The Dean had these letters run off, he just gave an order. Some rooms I add to my search are locked. Then I'm gone—to the next Entry—which is mine, casual with people near me, happening to follow me minding their own business, let them.

Paul's been to *my* room maybe about tonight. I'll play the new records, one is the musical *Street Scene.* I have only heard of it. They say it's an opera. The title sounds definite and passing. I pass people and am on my floor and at my door. The day is going, my knuckles rise but it's my door. Someone didn't lock up. My roommates have been and gone—to their late labs. I'm a busy thief if I take not a thing, I'm looking, I'm *seeing* it all, I'm home. The cigarette smell is closer, the pack in my shirt pocket feels nicely near-empty. My two hearts throb. I see my father wandering. The open door's familiarly behind me. I hold in my fingertips the two weightless, cellophane-enclosed large records in their vivid cardboard sleeves and let the store's white, monogrammed paper bag dive to the floor. A whole musical. Two whole concertos. I lay them on the closed luggage-like case of the portable phonograph. The roommate who owns it has left *his* letter on the bed. It speaks there on the plaid blanket. He's a bit nice but I like him, I trust his thoughts to be not much about me, his plans, his somewhat smiling diffidence in thinking prior to responding, male, true. He wants to read the letter again, I bet. I think I will tell him, I will tell him tonight.

I have the first page of his copy in my hand sensing his seriousness. I wish for my father's playfulness; it's all I want for a second. Someone is watching. It's exciting, this day. "So you're making the rounds," says Rush's friend in the doorway, resigned to the justice of what he has discovered.

He's got me. It's *his* cigarette. People have lost things. He's seen me, he could report it. Events are vulgar, I hear—I heard recently. But if he does not know what he's after, others like me may not know, yet maybe unlike them and him *I can.* "You've been into at least three other rooms, can't you find your own? You looked up and down the hall before you went in; why?"

If I'm about to harm him, he can't detect it, yet he hasn't enough to do and is threatening—but to do what? discount my father's letter? My father—does he hear my thought?—does his letter hear?—frowning/smiling at my mind, my father at the door of the smoke-rancid home of my room; my father's voice today everywhere but nowhere. I'm a virgin if that's the word, young for college, everything's up to me so long as I'll have anything I want. Be thorough, but about what?—about "a permanent impairment of my work habits"? I'm far from through with the wastebaskets: "a man easily diverted from his work by trivial matters has little chance of making an impressive contribution to his profession." "Three? Many more than three," I tell Rush's friend.

"Don't try coming into mine," he drones on. "People have missed things around here."

"Where *are* you?" I ask; "it's not this Entry, is it this dorm?" What is it that tries to catch my eye as I hold *his* eyes? "What would I have found there?" I needle. He says my name, the door ajar, I got his goat, he's going to step toward me, but doesn't. The guy in the white towel who flickers by in the hall is the one who talks to both parents at the same time on the phone. "Wait a second, I want to see if there's a note in my room," I say, so this person, in case he didn't know where he was, knows now—and I disappear: *Paul* won't have left a message; I have to find *him*.

"There's *this*," I hear Rush's friend say in the other room.

Had my father gone to Chicago and said No to his mother's "wishes," I would not be here, to say the least. My desk, my bed, my closet, my window, my bureau with the things on the top, the bureau scarf my mother had insisted on my taking, the toothbrush, toothpaste, a jar of Instant, and my Pickett's Charge shell nailed to its old block: I don't visibly see myself not surviving here, there are so many interesting and trivial things to do, I don't see myself doing much beyond coping (I have faith) with the demands of tonight. What's the thing I must do? Write my mother and tell her the letter looks good. Or phone her very soon after she gets in from work. Or *receive* a phone call *from* her (but I won't be here at nine or ten). Or let her stew in her own juice. Or tell her I could not say no to her. I lay out the four copies of the letter on my desk, moving my yellow pad with notes for my Poly Sci paper to the back edge against the wall where I've put up a shiny gravure magazine photo I cut out of Gandhi practically naked with some Moslems visiting from their own new country of Pakistan.

"There's *what*?" I demand domestically of the guy in the next room, and know; for it was what I almost saw while holding his gaze before, it was a piece of paper on the floor just inside the door—it was drawn in *along* the floor on an air current when I had first come in. Paul might have a car for tonight. But I did not imagine him bending down to slip a note under a door that was not locked; he would try the door before even knocking. Unless he didn't want to run into me. Having read my father's letter and recognized it somehow.

"This guy Manning." Rush's friend holds it out to me. "He says you should meet to discuss the letter." I took the note from his hand. There's a rhythm. Have we become sudden friendly acquaintances? I believe he's thinking, One has to toughen up sooner or later, and I'd be interested in knowing just what he means, or who.

He's got to get out of here, he says, humorous but he means it. He knows Manning's roommate from Alabama who's a terror, he says. I'm asking Rush's friend if he was aiming at me after class, flipping his cigarette butt along the path. Well, he thought that I was full of it, or something was up. *Up?* I said. You don't go around asking things, he said.

My father's real father, a lawyer, died when my father was ten. They lived in Brooklyn, my father was born in Manhattan, I have no rhythmic sense of it. An entire experience, having a stepfather, remembering his own father, or not remembering: I never reached an age to ask him about it: it was the stepfather that counted.

The phone is ringing at the end of the hall and the guy in the white towel trots past. I am asking things as if I'm leaving, both of us. I ask if he has a car handy; it's against the rules for freshmen, he remarks, but why?—do *I* have one "handy"? Not me, I think and say. I look at my watch. Is he having somebody up for houseparty weekend? Probably not, he ponders. He mentions the notorious college less than twenty miles away and I say I know some women there. He says he does too. I seem to want to dragoon him into something I'm running.

He said he was getting hungry, I looked at my watch. He said he had to eat every three hours, it was just something he had to do—it was in his *blood,* he said interestingly; sometimes he started to salivate like crazy. He put out his cigarette in the shining middle of the glass ashtray on the floor by my roommate's bed; rising, he snapped his fingers and in the same move pointed at the letter on the bed. He looked around, stared through into my room. I wanted to compare my four copies; I would ask him if he had his on him. But as if he has heard, he says that he read Rush's copy. Didn't *he* get one?, I ask like saying rather comfortably aroused lines. He didn't get to the P.O. I think of the irretrievable youth of my father. What thought is that? My father—he was seeing what would happen. He was spending his life on it. Living his responsibilities as they gripped and helped his heart.

The Post Office waste bins are being emptied within the hour, I imagine. *Rush's* copy, I think. What thought is that?

I asked what he would major in and he said Poly Sci or Ec. Ever read any Dostoevsky? *Heard* of him, is the reply, they stood him up but then didn't shoot him. But you haven't read his books? Nope. What're you going to do when you graduate? *Graduate?* he answers. He doesn't ask me. I'm curious, What did he mean Manning's roommate's a terror? Oh, he'll bend your ear about Alabama, he's going into politics, his father's a judge.

I asked what *his* father did. Private eye, Rush's friend said, evidently joking. I knew I had to go. What was on tonight? I asked. Rush's friend said he would try to understand biology tonight. How much room did we have here? he peered through the doorway of my small but more private and not *too* small room and took a look. He said he had asked for one of the few available singles well in advance, and I'm surprised but nod my head sagely. His parents said he couldn't; he has diabetes, they want him to have a roommate—so he's got *two*. I'm compassionately fascinated, does he have to inject himself? that's right is the reply, stalling my compassion.

As if he was looking for the way out, he asked if I was working this weekend, and I knew I had to know soon what Paul was doing. Did a car exist for tonight?—I would have to work to make this evening *happen*. I had a date, I said, and heard shouts gather down the hall. The guy in the towel who was planning to go to Germany next summer passed once more. Had I heard his voice on the phone?

It's another Thursday evening, Thursday poker, might as well be Friday, and the word has it that the Pope is easing up on Friday fish, the weekend tends to open swiftly and you don't want to let it get to be Monday yet, you could work all weekend. Rush's friend said that Manning's roommate had an opinion on everything, he was an old snake hunter, he would tell you anything you wanted to know. Rush's friend lifted one of my records in both hands to see the one underneath.

I looked at my watch and asked why he thought no son would have let that letter be used like this. If Paul's ride falls through, I might look up the chaplain's home phone number, I could tell his wife the truth. Rush's friend was leaving, he lighted a cigarette as if it would help him think. "All those copies of the letter on your desk," he said, "either you got extras or they're not yours. Did you change your mind?"

"But what did you think of the letter itself?" I asked.

Patient, Rush's friend took up my roommate's copy and sat on the bed to read it through. I heard his stomach. All the things my parents' friends may have said about the letter come to me along with their faces that are more or less looking at one other, two by two mostly. A noncommittal wry grin; a male shrug that's like a come-on to the inquiring spouse; a crass word or two about money, I hear opinions on love, seriousness, generosity; "he *told* me about this letter," I make up someone saying; the Oxford man with the pistols recalls a talk he and my father had concerning certain simi*lar*ities between Grant and Lee; and a future judge with a bit of a smile that I had seen on his mouth and cheeks often and felt was superior *and* shy so I felt stalled by this observation, observes, but with *poignant* judgment, that this couldn't have been said better. The faces, the speech mannerisms came to mind, to say the least as if they were in me. Naturally I wondered about my parents. I believed they had been happy. I want my mother to "know" what I feel, and writing *doesn't* deny the other a chance to answer, but she could phone, with those spaces, those pauses. I think about her—don't I? I see her anyhow: she gets home, she glances through the mail, the envelopes, puts them on the kitchen table while she runs water on the old ice tray, she either opens *my* letter and is instantly reduced to I don't know what, or she waits, she goes into the bedroom of the smaller but not small apartment we've (but now really *she's*) recently moved into: she sits to take off her shoes, puts her feet up—and sips her drink and cannot believe what she is reading in this letter of her smart, aggrieved, immature son, she *was* re*lax*ing.

He wanted to outlive himself. For my sake. It was kind and protective of him. He will never write me a letter here at college. He won't phone me either. Rush's friend reads and reads. I feel the fall outside, the wind to come, the movies downtown. I have two classes tomorrow. I see I must have bothered Paul at the restaurant not hearing him and that is why he is possibly receding in the direction of a girls' college along a curving sunset road.

I told Rush's friend I had to meet somebody. He let my roommate's copy of the letter drop gracefully on the blanket.

"It's like leaving a record of your voice," he said. What voice? I said, what voice did he hear? I tried to sound jaunty, Didn't we come here to get away from this parental crap?

Rush's friend was really going now. "You can't keep 'em from writing letters. This is somebody who—*I* don't know. It's a good letter, I guess. I've read it. I thought you had to go."

But he doesn't say it's my father; he doesn't say, *What did your father do?* Am I just any freshman creep? "All I can figure is that maybe this guy died," Rush's friend says; "that might be why his son would do this. If he didn't care about it, he wouldn't do this. But if he did care maybe he wouldn't. Do you think his father wrote this *before* he died and left it?"

Rush's friend said he was going to miss dinner and he would see me around. I said, "Of *course* he wrote it *before* he died, I mean..." and he laughed. He said to let him know if there were any women up there that he would like.

I shut the door and put on a record at 33 rpm. Why the "irretrievable youth of my father"? Gaiety and joking. Youth compared to others of his friends, who were pompous but his friends. Joking in the *family*: my mother, it was recalled with affectionate amusement in her presence (if not really much discussed), had been delivered of me nine months to the day after her wedding day.

I did something to the tone arm of my roommate's phonograph, lifting it off in the middle of the record.

I went to Paul's dorm. I did not *have* to tell anyone whose father it was. Paul's roommates had gone to dinner. I turned on the overhead light. If Paul had somehow recognized the letter as my father's, how had he? Sneakers and socks lay on the floor by the bed and the shirt and khakis he had been wearing on the bed and a black towel on the pillow and a T-shirt. There was a pounding of feet, and the Czech roommate flung open the door wrenching the doorknob simultaneously (it was what he did). Some girl had phoned for Paul. I said I believed Paul had a ride or had borrowed a car. The roommate smelled quite foreignly of after-shave. "Never mind," he said. He went into his room, came out and left.

My father's letter was standing up in Paul's basket, hardly a fold or wrinkle in it. I have not understood this letter of my father's. It is about *him*. Yet why not about me too? Or for me but not about me? And all this business we have done with his now tremendously altered letter the last year and a half, it is in my mind sounding and compressed radiating into its *own* unknown future. Into death, too.

They are moving out of the Quad in twos and threes to dinner. Roger, in a basketball jacket with its wide shoulders and trim neck, calls out to me, but I shake my head, waving.

I'm on my floor again going to see if I can run the tone arm through its cycle and unkink it. But the poker game that began this afternoon is skipping dinner, something in there hits the floor and a snickering is heard like some material tearing. The single room of the guy next door to the poker game who's going to Germany next summer is dark as I enter on impulse and hear the phone down the hall.

Dark areas of the room for a second grow from the amber glass shade of his gooseneck lamp which is standing on the flat arm of the old wooden chair, and the light bears downward—a little light on the subject—on a white envelope, the long business kind, and a folded letter lying on the scratched leather seat. I might as well sit down. There's a knocking down the hall and as I open out the letter which is not my father's I know I'm going to hear my last name called, and I do.

"Dear Guy," the letter begins,

After your call, we sat up talking upstairs until one a.m. We're tired this morning, but we haven't changed our mind. We have wished only that you would wait until you graduate to marry this girl. We assume we will meet her. We have given you all you could ask by way of support, and in our view you plan to throw it all away by marrying.

Freshmen who were veterans could be married, but not normal freshmen, but maybe the parents didn't know this because the letter asked what the two of them would live on, would the girl work to pay for an apartment there, but what kind of work could she get in a small town? What if she got pregnant, he would be stuck with a baby, the letter said, and what would become of his plans to become an architect?

I'm interested. I'm not really interested. What was the thing I must do? I'm interested in what I didn't know about him. I would not read any more of this and skipped to the end, the middle of the next page. It was signed, "Love, Dad and Mother." The room's dinnertime darkness flowed away and then toward me in the sharp, comfortable light of the lamp. I went back a few lines: "Your mother's about the same, holding her own"; back further: "you seem pulled irresistibly toward this tremendous mistake which will be an obstacle you can't begin to measure now."

I figured the parents would come around, at least pay the major bills. But was he going to Germany after all in June on a student ship? I did not see my father's letter but did not look. I saw the bedridden mother on *her* phone, the father, who I happened to know was a banker, downstairs. I was ready for some music but dreaded the tone arm not working. I was always starting up, it felt like—not in the morning only but at each hour and at moments of sudden testing in talk—with Paul, and with Manning, whom I didn't yet know—or at the moment of tipping the first beer of the late afternoon and thereupon seeing things a little differently. Why should Paul have an unused copy of my father's letter?

I smell apples and cigarette smoke in the darkening air, cigarettes anyway. A clock tower, probably the Gothic chapel, gonged, one stroke for each six of my steps.

Paul's copy was in his wastebasket, the Dean's pretentious little covering letter folded with it. I read looking still for some impression in the pages that made it Paul's letter. He would be interested at least in the fact that I was the mystery freshman, yet I didn't want him to know. Somebody knocked and I said Yes. I stood there and the door opened and it was a girl.

"Are you Paul?" she said. I said No (interestingly, I hoped), and she said, "You fool, why aren't you?" She's strong-looking, her hair a little over her face, her dark plaid skirt pulled tight across her hips and tummy, I look away from her breasts to her eyes. I told her where I thought Paul was.

"But he said there was a party here—right here," she said— "I just drove down from there, for God's sake, I could have worked tonight, I *never* use my car if I can help it, I hate it," she stuck her nose up (silly, mysterious, stupid, I'm nonplused), pursed her lips, and giggled. "He must have thought you weren't coming," I said. She leaned against the edge of the open door, swaying, and I saw her breasts soften toward each other. Paul had switched *ends* with her and was stuck up there where she had come from. It was a wonderful or miraculous relief to have her here. I thought of a friend's sister's closet, the shoes I had seen tumbled there in such personal haste, or evidencing that she was thinking of other things.

I said she was the one who wrote plays. One at a time, she said. When she found out how I knew, she laughed and said, *Now* she knew who this Paul character was—*now* she knew. But in order to ask who *I* was she ascertained that I didn't live in this dorm, I lived in another dorm, so she asked what I was doing here as if it would entertain her and I said I was reading this letter that was in the wastebasket, and she said Fair game.

Her teeth were somewhat large, they were thoughtful. She had a lovely narrow craggy nose, I thought. Her name is glamorous because I already know of her. Her name is Nina.

She sashayed independently around the room, she plucked things from here and there, putting them back, with terribly swift absorption she opened a new book so she cracked the spine satisfyingly, and I knew she could say awful things and was generous with herself. She looked into the two small rooms and came out again and looked at a snapshot in the corner of a mirror and stopped short, catching my eye. "Got anything to drink?" She wheeled to confront me, and I, upon experiencing a momentary blackout, on second thought shook my head. "Oh well," she said. "Oh shit," she said.

I felt we were doing two things at the same time, but what *were* they? "Oh *I* don't know," she said, her voice breaking, "I don't believe in wasted time," she said. "You don't believe it *gets* wasted," I said, amazed by her because I had once had the idea too. "That's it," she said. "I mean, here we are." She came and put her fingers on the letter. "Can I look at it too?" she asked. I realized she was smoking, her cigarette hand held far out so she seemed to use a holder. There was whiskey in her.

Nina asked me if I was *sure* I wasn't Paul. She liked me, or thought I was O.K. But No, she said, she vaguely remembered him from some evening up in *her* neck of the woods, very vaguely, she didn't have a picture of him. "I don't believe you," I said unexpectedly. She recalled his *voice* sort of, how he held forth that night, and when someone said Bullshit to him, *he* said right back fast, "That's-right": so you didn't know but it sounded as if he was throwing it right back as if the one who'd *said* "Bullshit" was referring to *himself,* not Paul. Was this *his* letter? Yes, I said. She took it away and sat on the bed on top of Paul's underwear and crossed her legs. She read for a moment. "Didn't you get one of these, too?" she said. She's read the Dean's covering note. I nodded. She read on, so I felt how much she liked her cigarette, the soft, busy currents of smoke pouring exactly through her nostrils and then a dollop out of her slowly opening and closing mouth. She looked up at me, but I didn't know what she was looking at. She thought about me.

"I should have had a father like this," she said, not sadly. "I mean I did have. I still do. In my mind." I asked if she meant he was dead, and she laughed, God no, still very much alive, oh boy *is* he! and still getting over the great time he had in Europe, three and a half years of excitement, English women officers, he was decorated, the works. And crazy about everything Nina did, in *his* eyes she could do no wrong, she'd actually tried and it was no use. Her skirt came above her crossed knee, she wore loafers and stockings that I imagined ending somewhere up beyond her knees.

I said my father had been rejected. But which was the father in her *mind* that she'd mentioned?

"*This* one." Nina shook the letter. "He keeps me going, he's on my tail."

"Are your parents divorced?" I said. What did I want from this girl? I wanted something.

"And did your father write this letter?" she said.

I said coolly, "*He's really* dead. But did you mean you had a second father?"

"No," she said, letting me delay, "just one, who adores me."

"And this other one?" I pointed at the letter in her hand.

"Oh he bugs me, that's all. He's not real, except sometimes I imagine him."

I told her that it was my father who had written this letter she held in her hand, and that I had let it happen, and I knew that it was partly just that, to let it happen, though I had felt I *ought* to, but now I had decided it was a stupid thing to have done. She frowned and smiled. "All those copies. Two hundred? three hundred? Better *not* think it was a stupid thing," she said. "But it wasn't *your* idea," she said.

"What if it was," I said, sniffing out her gentling tone—she might want to go, but she liked being here, she was honest. This wasn't the time for one of Paul's roommates to arrive. I said that it was a fine letter, of course. "He liked to talk things over. Man to man. I mean, he was a good talker. He could be funny," I said.

"Look at the ending, though," she said, reasonably moved by my words or me; she read it straight:

"If you occasionally have to give up something you desire greatly at the moment, try to remember that, however keen the disappointments of youth may seem, there is nothing—

I mean, listen to how this sounds," she said quickly, "it's a speech, for heaven's sake:

... there is nothing as bitter as a middle-aged man's realization—"

"Don't read it," I said. I wasn't incensed enough against her. What if one of Paul's roommates showed up? "*I* know what he said: '. . . a middle-aged man's realization that he doesn't amount to much.'"

She was watching me. "But how *could* you remember such a thing? You haven't had a chance to fail yet."

"We're reading it *today,* what he wrote, *we're* remembering him," I said.

"*You* are," she said.

If I was not incensed enough against her, enough for *what*? What might I do, what could I show her? The letter stood well and truly between us for us to talk about. I knew the words that followed: *Whatever else you have to endure, I fervently hope you will be spared this.*

"It's not funny," she said. "You said he was funny. It's a depressing letter, if you ask me."

"But *that* was certainly funny," I said—"I mean, how could *I* 'remember' that there's nothing as bitter as a middle-aged man knowing he doesn't amount to much. On the day I *got* the letter I had that thought."

"But it got written down," she said, and I had the simple thought that I was talking with someone about my father's letter. "A long time before he died," I said.

"And *is* it," she asked like an actress, " 'man to man'?"

"He wrote letters to me *after* this one; this just took longer to get to me," I said.

But she took me seriously: she asked how long. Nearly three years, I replied. "He kept it," she said. "I mean you got it. Even if he went back and worked on it, he liked it. And then in the midst of his death, here was his voice. 'Whatever else you have to endure.' "

"Yeah, I kind of wondered what he had in mind there," I said near her.

Did she ignore me? "You have to be someone to write something," she said. "Like this," she said.

"He *was* someone," I said.

"And this is what he wrote," she said.

"He wasn't *just* like this," I said; "good grief, *your* father and mother aren't the same all the time."

"He's pretty consistent. I hear him."

"Are your parents divorced?" I asked, like asking how many guys had made her.

"I hate to talk about it," she said.

"What is it that I 'have to endure'?" I said.

"Let's face it. It's not an affectionate letter," she said, continuing her own thought.

"What do you mean it's not an affectionate letter?" I said.

"I mean, I hate it. It bugs me," she said.

"You don't get everything at the same time," I said, not knowing what I meant.

"It's about *him*. But here *you* are," she said. She said I could dwell on the letter all my life, for heaven's sake. She said what about going someplace and having a drink.

Being a drinker and being intelligent as she was went together. "When he died, everyone said, 'Time heals all wounds,' but I didn't believe it," I said.

Her eyes were alert, mad. "Oh come on, not *ev*erybody said it." "Anyway, that's what I heard," I said. "It didn't heal *his,*" she said, and I wondered how she knew. "Except when he died," I said smartly. She laughed.

The night watchman could get me suspended. He went around listening for girls' voices after seven; just music on the radio would make him wait. I said it would be best if she left Paul's room after me. "What is it that I 'have to endure'?" I said. It was like thanking her too much. I felt naïve but had spoken.

In its time the letter calls me, advises me. To know what I could not know, could I? I'm not interested in being middle-aged. Yet I am still imagining these things in his absence. Like not *amounting* to much: now there's a line that will draw your effigy any time you want. I could imagine what a middle-aged body *looked* like—in motion, in some clothes, in a bathing suit, the knees, the hamstrings, the chest. But not what it felt like around you, with its effort, its bones, its cells. And for a second I could be older than my father.

She lighted a cigarette, it was like smiling. "You mean, what was *he* thinking of?"

But I didn't *want* somebody else's answer.

She was older. I said, "Would you go to bed with me?" I wondered where we would go. She looked at me, she was about to do something. "No," she said. She took my temples in her hands, she touched her mouth to my mouth twice, her eyes were almost shut, and then a third time. Some taste went away from her breath, maybe into me, and I smelled shampoo in her hair. "No," she said with attention to me and to herself all at once, "certainly not."

"Certainly not tonight," I said wildly.

"Certainly not tonight," Nina said, unlike any girl I had ever talked to. I had never said such words as these; they were a little false, I knew. "What's that guy look like—Paul?" she asked.

I was about to describe him, but I told her I didn't believe her. She said I was probably right—it was the rest of him she didn't remember. But I asked her to tell me what he looked like. She did, as in the most intimately pleasant game. "I had a snootful that night," she said. I returned the letter to the wastebasket. She is talking about where to go, and, as if to make sure her response to my crazy question was very clear, answering again, "No, but I'd like a drink if you don't have anything here." Nothing is accomplished. Or I haven't done the thing I thought I knew when I saw the albino in the Post Office and reflected upon him and his swarthy co-worker. I thought it would not be done, whatever I was supposed to do, until it came to me. What was I being spared? Did my dad know how I would take his letter? I won't answer for him. I insulted him on the street, and I still didn't know why but I want to mention this to Nina, an unthinkable insult coming out of nowhere—he hadn't been much of a drinker, where had the words come from? Things are blessedly incomplete.

I said we would go downtown and get something to eat. I had to go to my room. She told me which was her car. She looked at me, and I went back and hugged her, and she didn't move her hips back. My hands, my fingers, came up her back to curve forward upon her shoulders. "Is you a fatherless child?" she said. "Not me," I said.

It's Thursday, freshmen are returning from dinner, a shout in the Quad, the mountain where it was. I found a note stuck in my door as I instinctively deciphered sounds of the poker game nearby. "A woman" had phoned. The other call scrawled on the scrap of paper was the chaplain, for heaven's sake. I found that my father's letter had been taken from my roommate's bed. If I am not going to get laid, would I rather talk to Manning, that weirdly formal Manning?

I did not wish, really, to go into the honeymoon story my mother had told me—my father getting letters in Bermuda from his mother during those ten days telling him how much she missed him. What would Nina say? When exactly did my father move the letter from the safe deposit across the river to a lower drawer of the old drop-leaf desk? When he journeyed out to see his once-upon-a-time-widowed mother Christmas night, did he think it might be her last Christmas to see *him*? I would speak of how I had let this letter business happen, because Nina would ask. I would tell her this was not the first time. I took my checkbook and thought of my classmate who had shown me how to write a check. Will I know more about my state? I am wild, in my haste, and I will live a new life. The letter is everywhere and I can't answer for it. I'll answer the letter. I can't. But I will.

A NOTE ON THE TYPE

This book was set in a digitized version of Granjon, a type named after Robert Granjon. George W. Jones based his designs for this type upon that used by Claude Garamond (c. 1480–1561) in his beautiful French books. Granjon more closely resembles Garamond's own type than do the various modern types that bear his name. Robert Granjon began his career as type cutter in 1523 and was one of the first to practice the trade of type founder apart from that of printer.

Composed by
Brevis Press, Bethany, Connecticut

Printed and bound by
Fairfield Graphics, Fairfield, Pennsylvania

Design by
Dorothy Schmiderer Baker